Lennox is a silent protector. He's more than happy to let his twin do the talking, but in this case, he can't, because he's met his mate, and he's the only one who can get to know Owen — which might be hard, because even Owen doesn't know himself.

Owen was adopted into the Springfield pack, but he never belonged. While he wasn't abused, his father made sure he knew he wasn't loved and that he knew something was wrong with him. He doesn't know what that something is, but it has to do with shifting, which he was forbidden to do.

Between Lennox and his new home, Owen finds the strength to go against his adoptive father's will and shifts. Instead of the monster he expected, he shifts into a special kind of wolf — a dire wolf.

But dire wolf shifters are said to be extinct, and if they aren't, how did Owen end up in Springfield?

Lost and Found
Copyright © 2020 Catherine Lievens
ISBN: 978-1-4874-3031-3
Cover art by Angela Waters

Published by eXtasy Books Inc or
Devine Destinies, an imprint of eXtasy Books Inc

Look for us online at:
www.eXtasybooks.com or www.devinedestinies.com

LOST AND FOUND
LEGENDARY SHIFTERS 4

BY

CATHERINE LIEVENS

CHAPTER ONE

The wolf shifter was Lennox's mate, and Lennox had no idea what to do with that.

They were in Springfield pack territory because Toby, the Rosewood alpha's mate, had been taken. Lennox had half a mind to burn down the Springfield pack, but he knew better. He wasn't the one in charge. Camden was, and he only had eyes for Toby. Lennox understood that, even though he didn't have a mate.

Well, he hadn't had a mate until now.

He still couldn't wrap his mind around it, but he knew it was normal. He hadn't known his mate until now, and he hadn't expected to, especially not in Springfield pack territory. He was here to threaten the Springfield pack, to make sure they gave Toby back, not to find his mate.

But it was a relief to find his mate and to realize he was coming home with them. Lennox didn't know why he was coming, and he wanted to find out. The Springfield pack was his mate's home. Why was he so eager to live with people he didn't know?

It made Lennox wonder, and he had a hard time focusing on what he was doing, which was protecting the alpha and his mate. It was why he and his twin brother had moved to Rosewood and why they were staying. Well, in part. Carey had found his mate, and he'd also gotten himself a boyfriend. Lennox hadn't been surprised. Carey was well-loved, and he'd always been the most outgoing of them both. Lennox didn't know if he was quiet because Carey was a chatty Cathy

1

or if Carey had become so chatty because of how quiet Lennox was, but it didn't matter. What *did* matter was that they weren't going anywhere. Carey surely wasn't, not with two men to take care of, and now, Lennox had met his mate, too.

"Lennox?"

Lennox shook himself and looked at Toby. "Are you sure you're all right?" he asked to hide the fact that he'd been day-dreaming.

Toby cocked his head but nodded. "They didn't hurt me. Owen made sure I was okay."

It took Lennox a moment to realize who Owen was. Then, he peered at his mate again. "That's your name?"

Owen nodded without looking at Lennox. "It is," he murmured.

Lennox didn't know if he was usually as quiet as Lennox or if he wasn't talking for another reason, but he hoped for the latter. If neither of them talked to each other, their relationship wasn't going to be an easy one. Of course, the fact that they were mates didn't mean they would have a relationship, but Lennox didn't want to think about that just yet. For now, they needed to take Toby and Owen back home, and that was what they were going to do.

"We should head home," Camden said, mirroring Lennox's thoughts. He was nervous, and he wasn't the only one.

They technically were in enemy territory, even though the Springfield pack alpha wasn't threatening them. Lennox wanted to take Toby and his mate away, and the sooner they did that, the better he would feel.

They climbed into the car, and Lennox kept an eye out for the Springfield pack. The alpha was still looking at them, talking to John Harris, the man who had taken Toby. Harris looked like his head was about to explode. But so far, the Springfield alpha was holding up his side of the bargain. He wasn't trying to stop them from leaving. He hadn't tried to stop Owen from leaving, even though he was his pack member. He was simply watching them, and he looked angry, but Lennox couldn't say if it was at them or at what his envoy had done.

Kidnapping members of other packs, but especially an alpha mate, was a big no-no. Lennox understood why Harris had done it. Toby was a unicorn shifter, and he had the power of healing with his hands. It was intriguing and lifesaving. The Springfield pack would no doubt have a healer, just like the Rosewood pack did, but unicorn shifters were different. They could heal in minutes. They could heal wounds normal healers were powerless against. Every pack or shifter group wanted one, and the Rosewood pack had two — two brothers. It wasn't a surprise that the Springfield pack had tried to take one away, not once, but twice. Harris even had the balls to come into the Rosewood pack territory and take Toby, and now, he was going to pay for that.

Lennox hoped the Springfield alpha wouldn't change his mind. It would mean war between their packs, and no one wanted that, especially not the Rosewood pack. Even with Lennox and Carey there protecting them, it would still be hard on them. They weren't equipped to go to war with another pack, especially not a big one like the Springfield pack.

There was also Owen to consider. The Springfield alpha probably wouldn't have allowed him to come with them if he had decided to wage war, but they couldn't be sure. They had to be careful, just like they always were, maybe even more so. Toby was safe, and Lennox doubted Camden would allow him out of his sight for a while, but he wasn't the only rare shifter who lived in Rosewood, and that meant Lennox and Carey had to keep an eye on all of them.

Lennox was relieved once they closed the doors and Camden started the car. He held his breath, waiting until they left Springfield territory. Then he allowed himself to relax and peek at his mate.

Owen was sitting in the back seat next to him. He didn't seem to have realized they were mates, which meant he probably hadn't smelled Lennox yet. Lennox wanted to lean closer, to make sure that happened, but he didn't want to make Owen uncomfortable. He had no idea why Owen had decided to leave the only home he'd probably known in his life behind so easily, but something told him it wasn't a pretty story.

Besides, now wasn't the moment to talk about it.

Lennox moved closer to the car door. He was pretty sure he looked ridiculous, plastered like he was against it, but it was the only thing he could do. He had so many questions, and he wanted Owen to answer them. He didn't want to ask them, though. He didn't want to make Owen uncomfortable, or rather, he didn't want to make him even more uncomfortable than he already was. It was obvious from the way he fidgeted, from how he kept a hand on the car door as if he expected he would need to jump out at any second.

Toby twisted in his seat, and his focus moved from Owen's hand to his face. He seemed to realize the same thing Lennox had been thinking, and he smiled softly. "I know you're worried, but you'll be okay. I promise. You helped me get away from John, and it means a lot to me."

"I'm pretty sure you would have gotten away from him on your own, even if I hadn't been there," Owen said. His voice was musical but soft, and it made Lennox's stomach churn in the best of ways.

He knew it was ridiculous, but he could imagine them together, creating a relationship, maybe a family. He was getting ahead of himself, though. He didn't even know if Owen would want him. He had to keep his thoughts and his dreams in check, at least for now. They had no idea what had happened to Owen, but if Lennox was sure of one thing, it was that something *had* happened to him. There was no other explanation for his eagerness to leave the Springfield pack behind, and Lennox hoped that eventually, he would find out. He wasn't usually one for revenge, but he wouldn't hesitate to sic Carey on the Springfield pack if they'd hurt his mate.

He noticed Owen looking at him. He forced himself to smile, something he didn't often do, and Owen's eyes widened before he looked away. Lennox berated himself. He'd managed to scare his mate just with a smile. What was he going to do? He wasn't one for relationships. The only person he was close to was his brother, and that was only because they were twins, and they'd grown up together. How was he going to talk to Owen? What was he supposed to say and do? What were the odds that he and Carey would both find their mates while staying with the Rosewood pack?

Apparently, they were high.

Owen couldn't breathe. He'd never done anything like this. He'd never strayed away from the Springfield pack, not since he'd been adopted into it when he was a baby, and now, here he was, leaving and planning on staying away.

What had he been thinking? He hadn't even taken his things with him. He'd left everything behind, and he knew better than to think that John would make sure he got them. Hell, his father would probably burn everything to the ground and dance around it like an asshole. It would be just like him to do something like that, although maybe he wouldn't have the chance. Alpha Johnson looked angry enough to beat Owen's father into the ground, and Owen wouldn't be surprised if that happened. Even if it didn't, his father would pay for what he'd done, just like he ought to.

Owen still couldn't believe what his father had done. Had he thought it would work? Had he thought the Rosewood pack would stay away? They couldn't have, not when he'd kidnapped their alpha mate.

Or maybe he hadn't been thinking. Owen knew better than anyone how his father was when he was angry, and he'd been pissed at the Rosewood pack. They'd fought him, threatened him, beaten him. He'd told Owen that one of the phoenix shifters had threatened to burn him, and he hadn't taken it well. Obviously, he'd come up with his stupid plan after he'd come back home. Even though Alpha Johnson had told him to stay away from Rosewood, he hadn't, and now he'd made a mess.

Or maybe it wasn't really a mess. Whatever he'd been thinking, he'd given Owen this chance. It was terrifying not to know what would happen and what he was going to find, but for the first time since he'd been adopted, Owen was free. He was leaving Springfield behind, and the future was as exhilarating as it was terrifying. Whatever happened, it couldn't be as bad as the Springfield pack and having to live with his father.

"Are you sure you're okay?" Toby asked.

Owen forced himself to smile. "I'll be fine."

"We can go back, if you want."

"I don't want to go back. I wouldn't have come with you if I had doubts."

"Are you sure? I was pretty heavy-handed with you. I don't know why you helped me, but you don't have to come with us if you don't want to."

Owen had felt compelled to help Toby get free. His father had been keeping him chained in the basement, and it wasn't right. He would probably have been able to hide Toby from his mate and the rest of the Rosewood pack for a while, but Alpha Johnson would have eventually found out. That was still too much time for Toby to be chained to the wall, and Owen had made the decision to go against his father. He'd unchained Toby and had told him his mate was there for him.

He'd been stunned when his father caught them and Toby had reacted the way he had. He'd expected Toby to shrink back like he always had growing up, but instead, he'd fought back. He'd kicked John's ass, and Owen had watched in awe.

Then Toby had asked him if he wanted to go with him. He'd promised him he would be safe, that he didn't have to stay with the Springfield pack. For a moment, Owen had thought he was making fun of him in the cruelest way. But then he'd looked at Toby, and he'd known he could trust him. They barely knew each other, but Owen had met his share of people he couldn't trust, and he didn't think Toby belonged to that category. He was an alpha mate and a unicorn shifter. He probably knew better than most how cruel the world could be.

And he'd still decided to take Owen home with him, to free him from his father.

He'd never belonged with the Springfield pack, and he hoped things would be different in Rosewood. If anything, he was pretty sure the Rosewood pack wouldn't go around kidnapping alpha mates. That was more than good enough for him.

"No offense, but you don't look one bit like your father, and that's a good thing," Toby said.

Owen blinked at him. He had the feeling he'd missed part of the conversation, and he wasn't surprised. He was too deep in his thoughts, and that needed to stop. He might trust Toby, but even he knew that was probably stupid, and he had to be careful.

Even though everything he'd heard about the Rosewood pack was good, he had to make sure they wouldn't use him like his father had been planning on using Toby. Of course, he wasn't a unicorn shifter, so they wouldn't have any use of him, not in that sense. They could try to use him against the

Springfield pack, though. That was the last thing Owen wanted. He might never have been happy with them, but it didn't mean he wanted them to hurt. Most of the Springfield pack members were good people.

Owen cleared his throat. "I'm adopted," he explained.

"That explains a lot of things," Toby mused.

Owen nodded, but now that he'd been dragged out of his thoughts, he couldn't help but notice the man sitting next to him in the back seat. The man hadn't said anything yet. Owen didn't even know his name, and he wished he did. He wasn't sure what it was, but he wanted to move closer, to snuggle against the man. He'd never felt quite this way, and he didn't know how to explain it.

The man was beautiful. He had long blond hair tied behind his neck in a neat braid. Owen couldn't help but wonder how it would feel against his skin and how it would look un-braided. Then there were the blue eyes that were looking at him. It felt as if they were looking right through him, seeing his dreams and his thoughts. It made him want to squirm in his seat, and he had to resist the urge to do just that. The man also had a beard that was just as blond as his hair. It made him look a bit rough, but Owen didn't mind. He still thought the man was beautiful, and he wanted to get to know him.

He blinked. He had to focus before they got to the Rose-wood pack territory. He didn't know what he would find there, but he knew better than to be distracted, even if it was by a gorgeous man.

He turned his attention back to Toby, who was looking from him to the man with an arched brow. "John adopted me when I was a baby," he explained. "He's never been a great father, though, especially after my mother died."

Toby's eyes narrowed. "He abused you?"

Owen shook his head. "He never hit me, if that's what you're asking. He just never treated me like a son. It was always obvious that I was adopted, even to me. My mother loved me, though, and I always thought she was the only reason John allowed me to stay. After she died, things went bad. I didn't have a reason to be there anymore, but he couldn't exactly kick me out, not when the entire pack viewed me as his son, or at least, as the closest thing to a son I could be."

"Well, you don't have to worry about that anymore. You're wanted now. We want you in Rosewood, and I'm happy you agreed to come with us."

Owen hesitated. He wanted answers, but how would Toby react to his questions? "Why?" he asked anyway.

Toby wrinkled his nose. "I'm going to go on the assumption that you're asking why I wanted you to come with us."

"I am. I don't understand. You don't know me. I could be just as bad as my father." That probably wasn't the best thing to say. "I'm sorry he kidnapped you. He should never have done it."

Toby waved Owen's words away. "Don't worry about it. I know you're not like your father. Hell, he's not even your father. But you had nothing to do with the kidnapping, and the reason I wanted you to come with us is that I could see you weren't happy. I could tell you were afraid of your father. You still freed me, and you told me how to leave. You told me how to find my way back to my mate, and I'll always be grateful for that. It's one of the reasons I asked you to come."

"One of the reasons?"

"I could tell you weren't happy. We all deserve to be happy, including you. I wanted you to have a chance at that."

For some reason, Owen couldn't resist the urge to look at the man next to him as Toby spoke of happiness. Their gazes met, and he couldn't look away. He didn't want to. He had no idea what that meant, but he lost himself in the man's eyes, and he hoped he would never have to leave him behind.

Lennox didn't like that Owen hadn't been treated well. He also wasn't surprised. He was grateful to hear that Owen hadn't been abused, although abuse wasn't just physical. From the sound of it, Owen had been unhappy with the pack. He'd been unhappy with his father, even though the man had adopted him. He hadn't been loved, not by John, and he'd lost his mother. It couldn't have been easy for him, and since he'd said he never felt like he belonged with the pack, maybe it was right for him to move on.

Lennox couldn't make any promises, but he knew how Owen felt. He himself hadn't belonged anywhere until he'd arrived in Rosewood. Even there, it hadn't been easy. Lennox wasn't one who made friends easily. Hell, his only friend was Carey, and they were brothers. But he'd hoped that he would have another chance in Rosewood, the opportunity to live his life the way he wanted to, to find someone to love, to build a family.

And now, he had. He'd found Owen, even though Owen hadn't yet realized they were mates. Lennox had found people who wanted him in their life, no matter how surprised he was at that. They didn't care that he didn't speak much. Toby, for example, had pushed himself into Lennox's heart even though when they spoke, Lennox's contributions were usually grunts and nods. Lennox would make sure nothing happened to Toby because he cared about him, just like Toby cared about him.

It felt odd but good.

Both he and Owen had a chance at something better. Even if they were never together, if Owen didn't want Lennox that way, they would both have a better life than they'd had before arriving in Rosewood. It looked like Rosewood had a tendency to take on strays, and Lennox was happy about it.

He kept peeking at Owen as Owen talked. He couldn't help

it. He'd been shocked when he'd realized the wolf was his mate, but now that he'd had a few moments to come to terms with that, he couldn't help but stare. It wasn't like him, but then, he'd never met his mate before.

Owen was gorgeous. He was how Lennox had imagined his mate would be, which again, wasn't surprising.

They were very different. Lennox was fair, with blond hair and blue eyes. He was tall and broad-shouldered, and he had a beard. Owen, on the other hand, was shorter and slighter. He also seemed to be younger, but not by much. His hair was black, or as near to black as Lennox had ever seen hair. His eyes, too, were dark.

They would be a sight in bed, pressed against each other, their hair and limbs tangling. Lennox couldn't wait to see it, but he didn't want to spook Owen, who already seemed frightened enough as it was. Lennox had to keep a handle on his feelings and on his phoenix, who wanted nothing more than to cuddle up to their mate.

He wondered if Owen had realized they were mates by now. Maybe not, from the way he was behaving. He kept peeking at Lennox, too, his long lashes fanning on his cheek every time he looked down. He seemed like he didn't quite know what to do with Lennox, and at this point, Lennox wasn't sure what to do with himself, either. He wanted to drag Owen into his lap. He wanted to bury his face against Owen's neck, to give in to his phoenix's demands. Hell, he wanted it as much as his phoenix.

But Owen had just changed his life entirely. He'd left his pack, and even though he'd been unhappy with them, he still had taken a step into the unknown. It couldn't be easy, and if he didn't know Lennox was his mate, Lennox wasn't going to push. He couldn't, not if he wanted to make sure Owen wouldn't get spooked and leave.

What would happen once they were back at the Rosewood

pack, though? Owen would need time to get used to his new life. Lennox was more than happy to give his mate time. He wanted Owen to be aware of the bond they shared, though. Even if nothing happened between them in the beginning, or later, Owen had to know. He deserved to have all the information so he could make decisions.

Lennox didn't know how to do that. He didn't know if he would be able to get the words out. He had trouble with that the best days, and now he was even more emotional. He was floundering, and he wasn't used to feeling like that.

He wasn't good at talking, and he didn't want to make a mess of things. Owen was important, maybe the most important person in Lennox's life. Carey had been until now, but Carey had known Lennox all his life, so he wasn't offended when Lennox communicated with grunts and gestures rather than words. With Owen, Lennox would have to find another way.

Owen didn't know him. He couldn't read him the way Carey did, and that would be a problem. It was a problem that was easy to deal with, or at least, it would be easy to deal with for anyone but Lennox. He was getting anxious just from the thought of talking, though, and he didn't know what to do with himself.

These were the moments in which he wished he was more similar to Carey. Carey had never had a problem talking to people. Hell, once he started, you couldn't get him to shut up. Lennox, on the other hand, had always been anxious. He didn't want people to look at him. He didn't want people to talk to him. He felt better left alone, except for Carey and the people he cared for, which so far had been virtually nonexistent.

Things were different now. He would have to talk to Owen, if anything to tell him they were mates, unless Owen realized that on his own. The thought of talking to him made

Lennox's mouth dry, but he would have to do it. He was *ready* to do it. If Owen decided he wanted to try having a relationship with Lennox, Lennox would eventually have to talk to him. They couldn't be mates without talking to each other.

It was going to be hell as much as it was going to be heaven, wasn't it?

Lennox swallowed and kept staring at Owen, even though he realized he was probably making him uncomfortable. He didn't like it, but he couldn't seem to look away. Thankfully, Toby was distracting Owen enough that Owen peeked at him only a few times. Every time he did, Lennox forced himself to smile. He might not be used to this, either, but it was easier than talking.

And Owen smiled back. Every single time, the corner of his lips curled up. He always looked away quickly, but he didn't seem to mind that Lennox was staring, and Lennox was relieved.

He wasn't one for relationships, and now, he partly regretted it. He wished he knew how to deal with this, what to do. Carey wouldn't have a problem. Hell, he *hadn't* had a problem. When he'd met his mate, he'd realized the man was in love with someone else, and he'd taken it in stride. He'd decided it was a good thing because it meant he would have two boyfriends instead of one, but Lennox hadn't been sure about it. Carey, Sage, and Reece were making things work, though, and they were happy. If Carey could have that, if he could have his mate *and* a boyfriend, surely Lennox would manage to talk to the most important man in his life?

Lennox didn't know, but he hoped he would. He owed it to Owen, if not to himself. And once Owen knew what was going on, he would be able to make decisions. Even though Owen had come away with Toby and Camden and had told the Springfield pack alpha that he was moving in with the Rosewood pack, that didn't mean he had to stay there. He could leave anytime he wanted, just like every other pack member.

Lennox didn't know what would happen in the future. He wanted to know. He wanted to be sure he wouldn't be hurt, that he wouldn't lose Owen. He couldn't be, and that made him even more nervous. He was going to have to talk to Owen, and he hoped he would manage without panicking.

Owen was on the edge of panic by the time the car stopped. He couldn't go back, but he was terrified of going forward.

He shouldn't be. Toby had been nothing but kind to him, and even though Toby's mate, the Rosewood alpha, and the other man in the car hadn't spoken much, Owen didn't feel threatened by them.

He could be wrong. He had been before. But he didn't feel like they were a threat to him, and he hoped he wasn't wrong. He wanted this to work, even though it was crazy. He wanted the Rosewood pack to be his new home, and he prayed that was what would happen. He would have to get over his fear, though, and he wasn't sure he could.

He knew his eyes were wide as he climbed out of the car. For some reason, he wanted to get back inside. He'd felt calmer there, maybe because he already knew Toby, even though he didn't know him well. He'd felt comfortable, excited, and wary, but now he was in the open, and he didn't know what to do.

Two men rushed closer as soon as they saw them. One of them almost tumbled off the steps when he came down the porch, but the other held him up, and the pair moved toward their group.

Owen held his breath, but they ignored him, instead fussing over Toby. One of them looked so much like Toby that Owen didn't have a doubt they were related. He didn't know who the other one was, but they were obviously good friends, and it made Owen both envious and hopeful.

Maybe he could have this, too. He'd never really had a friend. Even when he'd been a child, most of the other wolf shifters in the pack had avoided him. He didn't understand why, although he suspected it had to do with his father, or maybe because Owen was forbidden to shift. For whatever reason, his wolf was a monster, or at least that was what Owen believed. Maybe the other wolf shifters could feel it. Maybe the shifters in Rosewood would feel it, too, and they would tell him they'd made a mistake, that they couldn't take him in.

He swallowed. He had to keep his mind off that. He couldn't show the Rosewood pack he was afraid or that he wasn't normal, not yet. Maybe later, if they accepted him. But right now, he had too much to lose.

He looked around. The pack grounds looked very much like the Springfield pack. They were both in the middle of the forest, with houses scattered around a small clearing. People were peeking from the windows, sitting on the porch, kids playing around, some in their wolf form, others in their human form. It felt like home, even though it wasn't, and that helped Owen relax.

Not entirely, though. He made sure to stay away from Toby and his friends, but he found himself at a loss. Camden, his new alpha, was talking to someone, possibly his beta. One of the twins was talking to another man, and from the way they leaned toward each other, he suspected the man was his mate, or someone just as important. That left Owen on his own, or rather, it left him with the man who had ridden with him, Toby, and Camden.

They hadn't been introduced, and they hadn't even talked, but Owen knew him more than he knew the people who were peering at him from their windows, so he moved closer. Even if the guy decided he wanted nothing to do with Owen, Owen doubted he would say anything to his face.

The wind played with the man's long blond braid, and Owen wished he had enough courage to ask him for his name. He moved even closer and forced himself to smile.

That was when he smelled it.

He looked around for a moment, wondering where the smell was coming from. He'd never smelled anything like that, and he'd never felt this way about anything. He knew what it was. All shifter children were taught how to recognize their mate, and he knew that was who he was smelling.

Owen's mate was a member of the Rosewood pack.

He felt his knees buckle, but he managed to stay on his feet as he continued looking around. From where the wind was coming, it wasn't hard to guess who his mate was, and he couldn't believe he hadn't realized it before. He'd been riding with his mate next to him in the car. How had he not smelled him?

Owen looked at his mate. Maybe his mate hadn't realized, either, and that was why he hadn't said anything. Or maybe he *had* realized, but he'd given Owen space. He might also not want Owen. Maybe Owen wasn't his type.

Owen didn't know what to think, but he had to stop freaking out before he had a panic attack. His mate hadn't said anything to him, so he shouldn't assume his mate didn't want him. Maybe he truly hadn't smelled Owen. The car windows had been open after all, and there had been another two people in the car with them.

He moved toward his mate, ready to ask for his name, but that moment, Camden stepped toward him. Owen forced himself to stop and looked at his new alpha.

"How are you feeling?" Camden asked.

Owen forced himself to smile. "Fine. Confused and bewildered, but I'll be okay."

Camden nodded. "That's normal. But if you're not sure you're okay, I can call our healer."

"I'll be fine. It's just a lot to process."

"I understand. You're shaken. You don't have to worry about anything, though. I don't know what your story with the Springfield pack is beyond what you told us in the car, but you don't ever have to go back if you don't want to. Alpha Johnson was clear about that. As long as you want to live here, you're a member of the Rosewood pack."

Owen didn't know what to say to that, except, "Thank you."

"You have nothing to thank me for. If anything, I should be the one thanking you. You helped my mate when he needed it, and I'm more than happy to welcome you in my pack. You can stay in one of the guest rooms in our house."

"I don't want to be a bother."

"You won't be. You're not the only one staying with us right now. Lennox is, too."

Owen looked around, trying to understand who Lennox was, and Camden pointed at his mate.

"That's Lennox," he explained. "He and his twin Carey are phoenix shifters, and I asked them to come here to protect my mate and his brother. They did a good job. Carey moved out of the house, since he met his mate, and both of them and their boyfriend are living together. Lennox is still with us, though, and I hope that won't be a problem for you. He won't hurt you."

Owen looked away from Lennox. He had a name now, and Owen wanted to step closer, to talk to him. There had to be a reason Lennox hadn't talked to him yet, though.

Their gaze crossed, and for once, Owen didn't look away. He'd been taught all his life not to look up at people, to avoid confrontation, to stay away. His first instinct was to do just that even now, but it was different. *Lennox* was different. He wasn't just a shifter. He was Owen's mate, and that had to mean something.

"Lennox?" Camden asked, confusion obvious in his voice.

Lennox stepped closer and cleared his throat. "We're mates," he said, his voice rough as if he didn't use it often.

Camden blinked at him. "Really?"

Lennox nodded once, curtly. "Really. I realized in the car, while I think Owen only found out now."

"Well, congratulations."

"Thank you," Owen managed to say.

Camden looked around, and when Toby came closer, he opened his arms to him. He kissed the top of his head, and Owen's heart ached to have the same. He didn't know if he could, but this was his best chance. *Lennox* was his best chance.

"You can come inside the house if you want, but if you'd rather stay out here and talk with Lennox, you can do that, too," Camden said. "You're a member of the pack, and you can go anywhere you want. Obviously, don't go inside people's houses without knocking and without authorization, but if you want to explore, feel free to do it. Or if you want to come inside the house and take some time to yourself to gather your thoughts, you can do that, too. Pick whatever guestroom you want to stay in."

It was overwhelming. Owen had gone from having only John, who avoided talking to him on the best of days, to living with Toby and Camden—and Lennox. He didn't know what to do with that, but he would have to find a way to deal with it.

CHAPTER TWO

When Lennox opened his eyes the next morning, the first thing he thought about was Owen.

They hadn't talked yesterday. Owen had been too overwhelmed, and Lennox hadn't wanted to make things worse. They'd acknowledged they were mates, but that was it. Even after finding out, Toby had whisked Owen away to show him his bedroom and the rest of the house, and Lennox hadn't protested.

It didn't matter how much time it would take them to talk. They already knew they were mates, and Owen needed other people in his life. From what he'd said, Lennox doubted he had friends, and Toby seemed to want to become exactly that. Lennox didn't mind. Hell, he was happy for Owen. He'd gone from not having anyone to having Toby, and probably the entire pack—and of course, Lennox. It was a massive change for him, and Lennox didn't want to push forward, even though, as his mate, he wanted to. But Owen knew where to find him if he wanted to talk to him, which was why he'd left him alone.

He couldn't help but wonder if he should do the same today.

He wanted to talk to Owen, or rather, he wanted Owen to talk to him. When he thought about talking to him, his mouth went dry, and he wondered what he would tell him. They should probably discuss what they wanted from each other, but Owen might not know yet. Lennox wasn't sure himself, even though he'd had some time to think about it. He'd wanted to tell his brother, but Carey had disappeared with his mate and his boyfriend, and Lennox had yet to see him again. He knew that would happen soon, though. He had no doubt Carey knew what had happened. He might be chatty, but he was also wickedly observant, and he had to have noticed how Lennox looked at Owen. He would tease Lennox, which was okay, at least when it came to this. There were worse things than being teased for finding your mate.

Lennox stretched and got out of bed. Once he was done in the bathroom, he headed to the kitchen, still wearing his pajama pants and nothing else. He didn't think anything of it — he wasn't shy. He hadn't been living with Camden and Toby very long, but even though it had felt weird in the beginning, he was comfortable with them. In the beginning, he'd get dressed before leaving his bedroom in the morning, until Toby had rolled his eyes and told him it made him look like he'd slept in his jeans and t-shirt and that it had to be uncomfortable. When Lennox had pointed out he wasn't home, Toby had been pissed. He wanted Lennox to consider this place his home, even though they weren't related.

Lennox should probably think about finding his own house, just like Carey had, but Carey's move had been easy. Both his boyfriend and his mate had a home here in pack territory, so they'd only had to choose one of them. Lennox, on the other hand, would have to start from scratch. That was one of the reasons he was still living with Toby and Camden.

Another reason was that he liked living with them. They were friends, even though Lennox didn't talk much, and he'd never lived alone in his life. He'd always had Carey, and it was strange not to have him here. It wasn't something Lennox wanted to deal with, especially not right now. He didn't know what Owen would want, but he wasn't going to do anything until Owen was comfortable.

He walked into the kitchen and made a beeline for the

coffee pot. He filled three-quarters of the cup with coffee, then added four teaspoons of sugar, and turned toward the fridge to grab the milk.

Someone squeaked behind him, and he froze. He slowly turned, almost smiling when he saw Owen staring at him. He managed not to, but it was hard. He didn't want Owen to think he was making fun of him. Instead, he grunted. "Good morning," he said.

Owen cleared his throat and looked away. "Good morning. I didn't mean to bother you."

"You're not bothering me."

"Are you sure? Because I can come back later if you want me to."

Lennox shook his head. His first instinct was to communicate through grunts, but only Carey understood him when he did that. He had to talk to Owen, and considering the conversations they would need to have, he might as well start now. "You want coffee?" he asked.

"I can grab it. You take whatever you were about to take from the fridge."

Lennox obeyed. He might want to take care of his mate, but Owen was an adult. If he wanted to get his coffee on his own, it was his right to.

Lennox grabbed the milk from the fridge, filled his mug all the way up, then turned around and looked at Owen, holding up the milk, silently asking him if he wanted some. Owen stared at the mug in Lennox's hand, his eyes wide. Lennox knew why. He didn't care if people thought he was ridiculous for drinking coffee with so much sugar and milk. He didn't like coffee. It was bitter and strong. The sugar and milk helped, and Lennox wouldn't apologize for it.

Owen finally shook his head. Lennox put the milk back in the fridge, then leaned back against the counter and wrapped his hands around his mug. The first sip was heaven, and he closed his eyes. They flew wide open again when Owen made a little moaning sound.

Owen's cheeks flushed, and he looked away, no doubt looking for an exit. His gaze stopped on the door, and he took a step toward it

Lennox didn't want him to leave. "How did you sleep?" he asked.

Owen froze. Lennox half expected him to leave anyway, but instead, he answered, "Fine."

Lennox nodded. "What do you want for breakfast?"

"I don't eat breakfast. I just get coffee."

Lennox frowned. "That's not good for you."

"It's fine. I'm not hungry in the morning."

Lennox wanted to push. He didn't know if he should, even though breakfast was the most important meal of the day and all that. He rubbed the back of his neck. He wanted Owen to stay with him in the kitchen while he had breakfast, but that would be awkward if he was the only one eating, right? Lennox couldn't expect him to sit there and stare at him. Besides, even if Owen was ready to do that, how was Lennox supposed to ask?

He growled at himself. He didn't like being socially challenged. He wished he were more like Carey. Carey always did the talking, and it helped Lennox immensely. But now Lennox was alone, and he was alone with the person who would be the most important in his life if he was lucky. What was he supposed to tell Owen? He had no idea, and he was terrified of saying the wrong thing. He didn't want to hurt Owen or to embarrass himself.

"Oh, you're both up," Toby said as he walked into the kitchen. He beamed at the sight of the coffee pot and rushed toward it, and Lennox couldn't help but smile. Toby needed his coffee in the morning, and Camden knew it, which was why he always made sure there was a pot ready before he headed to his office.

Toby drank down half his first mug before turning to Owen and Lennox. "What were you two doing when I came in?"

Lennox looked away. He could feel his cheeks heat, and he hoped he wasn't blushing. He grunted, and usually, it would have been enough of an answer for everyone. Most people were afraid of him, or at the very least, wary. It wasn't just that he was quiet. It was also the way he looked. He knew he was big, and the beard probably didn't help make him look harmless. He'd never minded that, at least not until now.

But Toby was different. He rolled his eyes at Lennox, then grinned at him. "Use your words. I know you can do it."

Lennox smiled again. "I was just asking him if he wanted breakfast."

"Oh, I want breakfast. Will you cook those scrambled eggs you do so well?"

"If you want." Lennox and Toby had started having breakfast together a few days after Lennox and Carey had arrived in Rosewood, and they hadn't changed that habit yet. Carey had left, but since Camden went to his home office early and generally had things to do, Toby was always eager to spend time with Lennox. Lennox didn't mind. He was kind of lonely without Carey, and Toby filled that hole.

Lennox got to work making scrambled eggs, and while he did so, he listened to Toby reassuring Owen.

"Don't worry about him," Toby said quietly. "I know he looks big and mean, but he's really not. He's quiet, so if you want to talk to him, you should probably take the first step." He paused, and Lennox heard him slurp his coffee. "Actually, you should probably take the second and third steps, too. You'll get used to Lennox and his quietness, but in the beginning, it can be weird."

"I don't mind," Owen murmured, and Lennox's chest

squeezed. Maybe his mate really wouldn't mind at all how quiet he was.

"I'm sure you don't. Listen, Owen. You can talk to me, Camden, or even Lennox. We're all good listeners, and if there's anything wrong or anything you want, I want you to feel comfortable enough to ask us. I know it's weird to be in a new place. I was in your place only a few weeks ago. I didn't always live with the pack, and I want you to feel comfortable here and to make yourself at home, because that's what it is. We'll be your home from now on."

Lennox was grateful Toby was so welcoming. He'd behaved the same way when Lennox and Carey had arrived in Rosewood. He was a perfect alpha mate, even though Lennox knew he was still hesitant when it came to his role. He'd put Owen at ease, though, which was what Owen had needed. Lennox wanted to do the same, but how?

Saying Owen was overwhelmed would be an understatement. He had no idea what to do or even how to feel.

He was relieved, mostly. The Springfield pack and his father had never abused him, but they hadn't been his home, even though he'd grown up there. His father hadn't been a father, either. He'd always resented Owen for being there, for being what his wife wanted, for the fact that he hadn't been enough for her and that she'd wanted a child. Owen had ignored that for most of his life, but after his mother had died, he hadn't been able to. How little John cared about him had become obvious then, and Owen had been thinking about leaving for a while. The main reason he hadn't was that he didn't have another place to go. He'd always felt alone, but if he had left Springfield, he truly would have been.

But he wasn't. He was never going back, not if he could help it. He wasn't as alone as he'd thought he would be, though. He knew he'd been lucky, and he was thankful. He'd met Toby, and he'd managed to help him. He hadn't expected Toby to drag him back home with him, but he was happy that was how things had gone. He felt lighter, even though he was confused and hopeful.

The fact that his mate was in front of him right now probably helped, too.

Owen had no idea how to behave when it came to Lennox. He wanted to talk to him, but as Toby had said, Lennox was intimidating. Owen wasn't sure what made him so, but he suspected it was a mix of being so quiet and being big and strong. He hadn't done anything to scare Owen, and Owen doubted he would, but still. Owen wasn't used to getting to know people he'd never met before, and Lennox was special. He was Owen's mate, even though Owen didn't know what to do with that knowledge.

But he was safe, which was the most important thing. He had a new home, possibly friends. It was more than he could ever have imagined after leaving Springfield, and he wanted to make the most of it. He wanted Rosewood to become his home, but he didn't belong yet. He knew that would change — hopefully. Once people got to know him, he would indeed become a part of the pack.

A door slammed in the distance, making him jump. Lennox turned toward the open kitchen door, but before he could say anything, his twin brother strode in.

They looked alike, yet not. Carey wore his hair short, and he didn't have a beard. It wasn't just that, though. Lennox was painfully quiet, but he wasn't awkward, although he might be with Owen around. Carey, on the other hand, didn't seem to be able to shut up for more than a few seconds, which was overwhelming. Even though Carey and Lennox were twins, they were as different as brothers could be, and it amazed Owen. They seemed to be close, and it made Owen jealous, because he'd never had a brother.

Carey beamed at Owen. "Owen! How was your first night here?"

Owen blinked at him. He hadn't expected Carey to talk to him, although, maybe he shouldn't be surprised. It felt very much like a Carey thing to do from the little Owen knew about him. "It was fine," he answered.

Carey's smile widened, something Owen hadn't thought possible, considering he was already beaming. "Did you sleep in my brother's room?"

The sound of a ceramic object put down too hard on the counter made Owen jump. Lennox growled and glared at his brother.

Owen wasn't sure what to make of Carey's words. He could feel himself blushing. He was lucky that while he had pale skin, he didn't blush easily. Lennox, on the other hand, was different. His cheeks were flushed, and it made him look adorable, something that shouldn't have been possible, considering how big he was.

"Sorry for asking," Carey said in a tone that told everyone he wasn't sorry. "I was just wondering if the two of you had talked. I know I wanted to spend the night with my mate and my boyfriend when I first met them."

Owen blinked at that. "Your boyfriend?"

Carey gestured at the two men who had come in with him. They were already sitting at the table with Toby, and one of them wiggled his fingers at Owen. Owen didn't know what to do, so he wiggled back, and the man smiled softly.

"That's Sage," Carey said. From the tone of his voice, he was proud. Owen didn't berate him for that. "He's my mate. The man next to him is our boyfriend, Reece. You'll get used to it."

Owen had no doubt he would. He didn't care if Carey had a mate, a boyfriend, or four of them. It wasn't his business, and as long as those men were happy, he wouldn't make it his business.

"Ignore him," Reece said without looking up from his coffee. "He talks a lot, but mostly, he has nothing to say. You can ignore pretty much everything that comes out of his mouth."

Carey spluttered. "That's not true."

"Isn't it? Because so far, you haven't said anything important this morning."

"You didn't say that when I told you how I wanted to take you—"

One glare from Reece was enough for Carey to snap his mouth shut. Owen was curious, but he was pretty sure that whatever Carey had been about to say it was personal, and he wasn't about to ask.

It truly was incredible how different Lennox and Carey were. Even if they had dressed the same way and had looked the same, Owen and probably everyone else would have been able to differentiate them. There was no way one could mistake Carey for Lennox or the other way around.

"Breakfast," Lennox grunted.

Owen hesitated. He honestly didn't eat much at breakfast, but that was mostly because he never wanted to have breakfast with John, who took his time in the morning. Maybe things would be different for him here. Even if he didn't need much, he should probably stick with the others. It would be a step forward to becoming their friend and getting to know them, and that was the thing he most needed right now.

So he sat. He wasn't surprised when Lennox put a plate in front of him, but he was when he saw what a small serving was on it. He turned to Lennox, who smiled at him and shook his head.

Owen had told him he didn't eat breakfast, and he'd made sure Owen wouldn't have too much to eat so he wouldn't have to force himself to leave half the food on his plate. The thought made something in Owen's stomach flutter, and he couldn't help but smile as Lennox sat next to him at the table.

This he wasn't used to, either. Even when he had breakfast, it was always with his father, and they were silent, almost deathly so. John never had much to tell him, and the same went for Owen. The men around Owen now were different, though. They talked as they ate, teased each other, played around. It was incredibly different, but Owen loved it, and he couldn't help but wonder if this was what his life would be like now—full of people, of voices and sounds and laughter.

He didn't know how to deal with all of it, so he stayed quiet, and of course, so did Lennox. Owen didn't mind. He felt comfortable with the silence between them. He knew they would have to talk eventually, but it could wait.

About halfway through breakfast, he caught Toby looking at them. Toby was smiling softly, and when Owen wondered why, he realized that he and Lennox might not have been talking, but they'd be leaning toward each other. Their elbows brushed every time one of them moved, and when Owen reached for the coffee pot to pour himself more coffee, Lennox beat him to it. He didn't even let Owen touch the pot. He took care of him, putting only one teaspoon of sugar in the mug just like Owen had earlier. Even though he'd only seen it once, he already knew how Owen took his coffee. He'd been watching, always silent but very much there.

It made Owen smile. He didn't know what the future held, either with the pack or with Lennox, but he could tell it was going to be good.

Lennox had been planning on talking to Owen once breakfast was over, but as he tried to follow Owen out of the kitchen, Carey stopped him. He grabbed Lennox's arm, and Lennox growled at him. Carey was used to this, so it didn't bother him. If anything, his smile grew even wider and made him look annoying.

Well, more annoying than he already was.

"What?" Lennox growled.

Carey couldn't seem to stop smiling, but at least he let go of Lennox's arm. "I just wanted to talk to you."

"And it couldn't wait?"

"I don't know. Why should we wait? You have something to tell me?"

Lennox wanted to tell him to fuck off. He knew better, though. His brother already knew something was up, and telling him to leave him alone would make it even worse. Then Carey would start pushing and getting annoying, and Lennox couldn't deal with that right now. Besides, they were brothers. No matter how annoying Carey was, Lennox knew he loved him and that he wanted him to be happy.

He sighed heavily. It was irritating, but it was his life. He should be used to Carey by now. They were almost thirty, and they'd lived their entire life together. Besides, Carey was better at this, as the fact that he was in a relationship with two men showed. Maybe he could give Lennox some pointers so Lennox wouldn't embarrass himself or scare Owen off. Lennox wasn't looking forward to the conversation, but it might not be such a bad idea.

He looked around. The kitchen was mostly empty now, with only Sage and Reece still sitting at the table. They were talking to each other, their heads close, apparently not caring about Lennox and Carey. Lennox didn't know if it was the truth, but he *did* know his brother would probably tell them what was going on as soon as he was out of the room anyway.

He didn't mind. He might not be exactly comfortable with the two, but they were his brother's men, and he should get used to having them in his life.

He rubbed his face. "Fine. Something *is* going on," he

grudgingly admitted.

"And will you tell me what?"

"You already know what, don't you?"

"I want to hear it from you."

Lennox huffed but gave in. "Owen is my mate. I found out yesterday."

Carey's smile was so wide that it looked like it might hurt. "I'm so fucking happy for you."

Lennox shrugged, uncomfortable. "I don't know. I don't want to ruin everything."

"I suppose it's a possibility, knowing you."

Lennox narrowed his eyes at his brother. "Do you have anything useful to say, or can I go?"

"Don't go. Fine. I'll stop making fun of you. You need help?"

Lennox didn't want to admit he did, but this was Carey. "Maybe. I'm not sure how to talk to him."

"You just have to open your mouth and say the words, Lennox. I know talking isn't easy for you, but Owen of all people would understand that, and he won't care."

"You can't know that."

"Not for sure, no. But most people are okay with you not talking a lot, and we give you time to put your thoughts together and get the words out. Owen is your mate. Maybe think about what you want to tell him before you do, or something like that."

Lennox frowned. "You want me to write a speech?"

"Why not? It's not a bad thing. If it makes you feel more comfortable with talking with Owen, I don't see why you shouldn't. He might think it's strange, but if he's going to spend any length of time with you and with us, he'll have to get used to it."

"What if I fuck things up?" Lennox asked quietly.

For once, Carey took the question seriously. He reached

out and squeezed Lennox's shoulder, bringing them closer. He didn't hug Lennox—they'd long ago established that Lennox wasn't comfortable with that—but he didn't drop his hand, and his heat sank into Lennox's body. "I know you're scared," he murmured. "I was terrified when I found Sage, and I realized he already had someone in his life."

"You didn't look terrified." But Lennox wasn't surprised. Carey didn't like showing people he was afraid, and usually, he distracted them by talking a lot. It was what he'd done when it came to Sage and Reece, but now, both of them could see right through it, just like Lennox.

"So what if you mess things up?" Carey asked. "Owen is your mate. He knows you're awkward with talking already. He would have to be blind and deaf not to, even though you only met yesterday. I think he'll be lenient with you. Besides, he's new here. He'll probably be happy to have someone to talk to."

"He talks to Toby."

"Of course he does. You're different, though. You're his mate."

Lennox wished that made a difference, and while in a way it did, it also didn't make it easier for him to talk to Owen. When he thought about doing it, his heart raced.

His throat felt tight. He didn't know why he was this way. He wanted to change, but he didn't think he could. He never had.

Carey squeezed Lennox's shoulder again. "Look. It's obvious that even thinking about talking to him makes you nervous. Why don't you wait?"

"We're mates," Lennox pointed out as if Carey hadn't heard him the first time.

"I know that, and so does he. I'm not saying ignore him. I'm saying that you should try to get to know him as a friend. You need to have the mate conversation, but considering that he just arrived here, I'm pretty sure he'll be grateful for a bit of respite. Maybe ask him if he wants to come around with you, to see pack territory. He'll probably be grateful for that, since he has no idea where everything is and who everyone is. You won't even have to talk too much, and if you do, you won't have to talk about your feelings. Just be there for him, make it obvious that you care about what happens to him even if you don't say it out loud. It can take some people time to get used to you, but it doesn't mean it's a bad thing."

"How would you know? You tell everyone what you think of them."

"It doesn't mean it's not scary and that I don't wonder if it's the right thing. You just have to try, Lennox. Come on. You found your mate, and I want you to be happy. I know you can be. We sacrificed a lot to get here, but you, especially. You decided to stick around with me even though you didn't have a reason to."

"I had a reason to. You met your mate here. Did you think I was going to leave on my own?"

Carey shook his head. "Of course not. I wouldn't have blamed you for it, though."

Lennox didn't want his brother to feel that way. He reached out for the hand Carey still had on his shoulder and put his fingers on top of it. He squeezed quickly, then dropped his hand, but it was enough to tell Carey how he felt. Carey's smile was softer now, and he gently pushed Lennox toward the door. "Go talk to him. Ask him if he wants to shift in the forest or something like that. Make him feel like this is his home. Make him feel like *you're* home. I know things will be awkward in the beginning, but they'll work out. I prom-ise."

Lennox knew Carey couldn't make that kind of promise. He couldn't know how things would go. He wasn't wrong, though. Maybe it was too soon for Lennox and Owen to decide anything about their relationship. They should get to know each other first. Lennox wasn't Carey, and Owen wasn't Sage or Reece. They had to find their own way to a relationship, and one of them had to take the first step.

It looked like Lennox would.

Owen's bedroom in Camden and Toby's house was nice, much nicer than the one he'd had back at the Springfield pack. He hadn't expected much, considering the circumstances of his arrival in Rosewood, so he'd been surprised and touched.

Toby and Camden really wanted him here. They wanted him to feel comfortable, and like Toby had said, at home.

And it worked. Owen couldn't remember a night when he'd slept better. John had never hurt him, but that didn't mean Owen hadn't been afraid of him. John used to slam doors and yell when Owen didn't do what he wanted, which happened often. Owen wasn't the perfect son John wished he had. The only reason he'd taken Owen in when Owen was a baby was that his wife had wanted a child. Martha had loved Owen like she would have her own children, so things had been okay for a long time. Awkward, but okay.

Then she'd died, and things hadn't been okay anymore. But now here Owen was, in a bedroom decorated in light blues and whites, with a thick comforter on the bed and a mattress that felt like heaven, with people outside the room who actually wanted him here. He didn't know if he'd stay in this bedroom forever, but it would be the perfect place for him to settle down.

Owen wasn't surprised by the knock on his bedroom door. He *was* surprised to find Lennox standing on the other side of it when he opened, though. He'd expected Toby, and now he wasn't sure what to do or say. He shuffled his feet and looked at Lennox, waiting for him to tell him why he was there.

Then he realized how ridiculous that was. Toby had told Owen how quiet Lennox was and that he didn't usually talk to people, especially people he didn't know. This time wouldn't be any different. Why should it be? They might be mates, but they didn't know each other yet.

Owen smiled at his mate, hoping to make him more comfortable. "Is there a problem?"

Lennox shook his head. He opened his mouth, sucked in a breath, and looked away. Owen waited. He didn't know why Lennox wasn't comfortable speaking, but he didn't want to hurt his mate or to rush him. Whatever was happening, it wasn't like Owen had anywhere to be. He could take his time.

Lennox rubbed the back of his neck, then finally said, "I thought we could take a walk in the forest."

Owen couldn't help but smile at the invitation. "You mean you and me?" he asked to be sure.

"Yeah. We don't know each other, and I think we should change that."

"Because we're mates."

"Because of that, yes, and also because Rosewood is your new home. Don't you want to get to know it, too?" Lennox paused and frowned. "But you don't have to do it with me if you don't want to. Being my mate doesn't mean you have to be with me."

His words settled something in Owen's chest. He hadn't realized he was afraid to be forced into anything, but it made sense. He didn't know Rosewood and the pack members, so obviously, he was nervous around them, even around his mate. "Thank you for saying that. I'd be happy to take a walk with you."

Lennox smiled, and it made him incredibly gorgeous, so much that Owen couldn't look away, especially since he suspected that Lennox didn't often smile that way. He almost missed Lennox's next words, but he did hear them, and they made his entire body go cold.

"I thought we could shift and play around," Lennox said.

It was hard to breathe. Owen opened his mouth, but only a croak came out. It got Lennox's attention, though, and he frowned when he realized Owen was panicking. "Owen?"

Owen didn't know how to answer. He didn't know if he *could* answer.

He couldn't get out of this without letting Lennox know that something was wrong with him.

He forced himself to relax. Lennox didn't know what was happening, and freaking out was only making him more curious and worried. Owen had to get a grip on himself before something terrible happened. He breathed in and out a few times, then forced himself to smile at Lennox. "Thank you for the invitation, but I don't think I want to shift today."

Lennox frowned. "No?"

"I'm not comfortable with it."

Instead of reassuring Lennox, the words made his frown deepen. "Are you afraid that someone will hurt you? The pack is full of wolf shifters, and even though I'm a phoenix, I promise I won't hurt you."

Owen realized Lennox thought he was afraid of the reputation phoenix shifters had of being hotheaded and setting whatever they wanted on fire. He didn't want Lennox to think he was afraid of him, so he shook his head. "It's not that. I know you wouldn't hurt me."

"Are you sure? Because I realize we don't know each other."

The worry seemed to have made it easier for Lennox to speak, and even though Owen was relieved, it also upset him. He didn't know how to explain. He didn't want to push Lennox away before he even had a chance to be with him.

But eventually, if things went the way they should, Lennox would find out, wouldn't he? It didn't matter how hard Owen wanted to ignore his secret, how much he worked to keep it hidden. Lennox was his mate, and if they did end up together, he would find out. Owen would have to tell him. He didn't want to lie, not to Lennox, and not to anyone who was welcoming him into the pack.

Owen didn't want to do it. He didn't want Lennox and Camden to send him away. He didn't want to lose everything he'd just found, everything he thought he'd never have. It was better to do this now. At least if he lost everything, he wouldn't have had it for long. It would hurt still, but not as much as it would if he stayed here for months or years.

He swallowed, wondering how to say it. He didn't think there were words to explain. He didn't know himself what was wrong with him. John had never told him, no matter how many times he'd asked.

Owen had to find a way. Lennox was still there, staring at him, waiting for him to say something, and Owen couldn't seem to get the words out. He wanted to explain, but he didn't even know *what* he had to explain. At that moment, he hated John even more. John had never been a father, and this was one more way he'd shown that. He should have prepared Owen for this. He should have told him what was wrong. Instead, he'd ignored Owen's questions, and when Owen had pushed, he'd told him to stay quiet and that he would be kicked out of the pack if he ever shifted.

So Owen never had. He was a shifter who didn't shift, but no one in Springfield had ever noticed. They'd never asked for an explanation, but the Rosewood pack would be different. They would expect Owen to shift, and he couldn't.

How was he supposed to explain that to them?

CHAPTER THREE

L ennox could tell there was a problem. He wasn't sure what it was, and he had no idea what to do. Should he ask why Owen was freaking out about shifting? Or should he ignore it and just act as if he hadn't asked his mate to go on a run together.

In the beginning, he'd thought it was because he was a phoenix. People tended to be afraid of a phoenix, and with good reason, especially after they got to know Carey. Carey was a great guy, although Lennox might be biased since they were brothers, but he was also a bit nuts, especially when it came to burning things down. Was that the problem? Was Owen scared Lennox would hurt him?

Lennox never wanted his mate to be afraid of him. He didn't want anyone to be afraid of him, even though that was kind of his job. Owen wasn't just a guy, though, and Lennox wanted him to know he would never hurt him.

He shuffled his feet, trying to find the right way to let him know that. He supposed he should just say the words. "I'm a phoenix shifter," he began.

"I know." Owen paused. "And I'm not afraid of you, even though it probably makes me an idiot."

Lennox frowned. "Your life was flipped upside down, and you don't know what to think. That doesn't mean you're an idiot."

Owen shook his head. "I should've known."

"What I was trying to say is that while I might be a phoenix shifter, you don't have to be afraid of me," Lennox continued before Owen could sidetrack him. The words tasted like ash on his tongue, but they had to be said.

Owen didn't look as spooked as he had a few minutes ago, which was a good thing, even though Lennox didn't know how he'd managed to do that.

"I'm not afraid you'll hurt me," Owen said.

"That's good, because I won't. I know phoenix shifters have a bad reputation, but I promise you, we're not crazy, and we find no pleasure in burning things down."

Owen arched a brow. "Not even Carey?"

Lennox had to smile at that. "Okay, maybe Carey *does* find some pleasure in burning things down. Only bad things, though. I promise he's not going to attack you or anything like that."

Owen sighed. "You think I don't want to shift with you because I'm afraid of you."

It wasn't a question, but Lennox felt compelled to answer anyway. "I do. People are usually afraid of us. I understand it, even though I'm not happy about it."

Owen shook his head. "It's not that."

Lennox wasn't sure whether or not that was the truth. He wanted to believe Owen. Owen was an adult, and he probably knew what he was talking about. Still, Lennox took a step back, just in case. He wasn't surprised to see Owen relax as soon as he was further away, and that settled it for him. Owen was afraid of him, of what he could do, and that was why he didn't want to go outside and shift with him.

Lennox didn't know how that made him feel. Well, he *did* know that he didn't like it, but what now? How was he supposed to show that he wasn't a danger to him or to anyone who wasn't trying to hurt him?

"You stepped away," Owen said quietly.

"I know you said you're not afraid of me, but I doubt it's true," Lennox admitted. "I don't want to scare you even more."

Owen snorted. "I'm not afraid of you. *You* should be afraid of *me*."

That was unexpected, so much so that it took Lennox a moment to gather his thoughts. "What do you mean?"

Owen sighed and rubbed his face. His shoulders slumped, and he looked so defeated that Lennox wanted to help him. He wanted to do something for him, but what? He had no idea what was happening. He wanted to believe that Owen wasn't afraid of him, but so far, everything spoke to that.

"I said you should be afraid of me because you should," Owen said. "It's not that I don't want to go outside and shift with you. I'm sure you're gorgeous in your phoenix form, and I can't wait to see it. I think it's fascinating, not scary."

And there Lennox went, blushing again. He ignored it, though. He wanted to focus on Owen, because there was something Owen wasn't telling him. "You don't have to shift to see me in my phoenix form. I can be the only one shifting, if you'd rather not."

"I don't know if I can shift."

This entire conversation was surprising to Lennox. "What do you mean? You're a wolf shifter."

"I am. But I've been forbidden to shift by my father, and I've never done it, not since I was a baby, and obviously, I don't remember doing it then."

Lennox turned the words over in his mind. "Your father forbade you to shift."

"He did. I don't know what happened. As far as I can remember, he's always told me I shouldn't shift. When the pack shifted together and ran, I had to stay home."

"Why?"

"I have no idea. He's never told me, but he was afraid. I guess I'm not like the other wolf shifters. Maybe I would scare the kids. I don't know. I just know that I can't shift."

Lennox didn't know what to say to that. It was obvious to him that Owen thought he shouldn't shift, but he didn't think that was right. Shifters were made for it. Whatever Owen turned into when he shifted, it was a natural thing, and he shouldn't have been forced to hold it back. "He's never told you why?"

Owen shook his head. "Trust me. I asked him several times. When I was a teenager, I wanted to shift with the few friends I had. I needed answers. I went to him, and he didn't want to give them to me. One time, I snuck out. I thought I could shift, even though I hadn't done it in years." Owen laughed darkly. "Hell, as far as I know, I *can't* shift. What's there to say that I'm actually a wolf shifter? But anyway. I snuck out, thinking I was smart. I wanted to be like my friends, you know? So I went with them, and we headed to the forest."

Lennox waited for a moment, then, when Owen didn't continue, he asked, "What happened?"

"I didn't get to shift. I didn't even get to take my clothes off. My father found me and dragged me home. That was the one time I thought he was going to hit me."

Lennox tightened his hands into fists. "Did he?"

"No. Not even then. But he yelled at me, told me I was an idiot, that I had to be more careful. He repeated that I couldn't shift. When I asked him why he wouldn't answer, he told me this was how things were and that I had to respect the rules, period."

"So you have no idea what happens when you shift?"

"I just told you I don't. I might be a wolf, or a bear, or a cow. I might be human." Except he knew he wasn't, because he could feel his animal inside him, lurking under the surface.

Lennox shook his head and leaned closer. He could smell shifter on his mate, but he couldn't tell what kind. "You're a shifter. That much, I can tell you."

"Even so. It doesn't mean that whatever I shift into isn't dangerous. Or maybe it's just horrible. Maybe I'm not a normal wolf. Maybe I'm defective, and my father was ashamed of it." Owen shook his head. "Whatever it is, I don't want to risk it. I left Springfield. I don't regret it, but I don't want to lose all of this." He looked at Lennox, probably waiting for an answer, but Lennox didn't have one for him.

Now that his dark secret was out, Owen expected Lennox to leave. Why would Lennox want to be with him and to spend time with him when he didn't even know if Owen was actually a shifter — and if he was, what he shifted into? Everyone would understand if Lennox left Owen behind.

Owen had always thought his wolf form had to be defective. It was the only thing that made sense. Why else would his father not want anyone to see him when he shifted? For a while, he'd wondered if maybe he was too dangerous for the pack, but that didn't make sense. He was a wolf shifter. He had to be. Why would he be dangerous? Unless his wolf form was crazed, but that didn't feel right, either.

Owen could be wrong. He didn't remember ever shifting, so maybe he really did go crazy when he was in his wolf form. Maybe he was a danger to others, and that was why his father had kept him away, making sure he never shifted. Whatever the reason, Owen didn't think he was up to finding out. He didn't want to push Lennox away even further by telling him about this.

He wouldn't blame Lennox for deciding he didn't want to be with him, but in the back of his mind, he still hoped that wouldn't happen. Lennox didn't look like the kind of man who spooked easily, and maybe as long as Owen promised he would never shift, they could be together. Maybe Owen really could make Rosewood his home, even though he was different. He hoped so, but he needed to remember not to keep his hopes up too much. It would be too easy for him to get hurt if—when—they kicked him out.

He looked at Lennox, who was staring at him. Everyone had told him Lennox was very quiet, but just now he'd been speaking okay. He'd listened to Owen, had tried to reassure him, to comfort him. He looked uncomfortable, but Owen couldn't tell if it was because he needed to talk or because of the situation they were in. Whichever the answer, it made his heart ache. He wanted to be with Lennox. He wanted to at least try to be with him. Things might not work between them, but they wouldn't find out if they didn't try, and they wouldn't try unless both of them were okay with it—and Owen might have just given Lennox a good reason not to.

He didn't know what to do with himself. He had to be honest, but he was terrified. He didn't want to show it, but he couldn't ignore that feeling. It was as if he expected something to happen, for the Rosewood pack to kick him out, maybe to send him back to Springfield. He doubted they would do it happily, not with what he knew about Toby and Camden and the other people who lived here. Still, they might not have a choice, not if they found out about this. They might want to help Owen, but they wouldn't be able to do it if it would harm their pack. Even though they'd welcomed Owen, he wasn't a pack member, not really. They could still send him home, and that was the last thing he wanted.

"We could shift anyway," Lennox said.

Owen blinked at him—sure he hadn't heard that right. "You can shift." That had to be what he meant.

Lennox shook his head. "I meant both of us. We can go to the forest. No one will come after us. The pack is smaller than Springfield, but we have more territory, so we can run around without anyone watching us."

Owen's first instinct was to take a step back and shake his

head. "I can't shift," he repeated. He could hear his father's voice in the words, telling him he had to be careful, that he *couldn't* shift. It had been repeated to him again and again as he grew up, so now even the thought of shifting terrified him. He was actually relieved he hadn't succeeded the one time he'd tried with his friends. He didn't know what he would have done if he had hurt them, and he didn't want to hurt Lennox or anyone else. They'd all been nice to him, and he couldn't thank them this way.

Lennox raised his hands. He didn't touch Owen, but Owen thought he looked like he wanted to. "Listen," he said. He paused, swallowed, then continued, "I know you're afraid that whatever you can shift into, your wolf or whatever your animal form is, is somehow defective. You're afraid to hurt me."

"Of course I am," Owen snapped. He sucked in a breath. He didn't want to hurt Lennox, either physically or with his words. "I can't risk it. Don't you see? There has to be a reason my father didn't want me to shift, and it can't be a good one. I must be defective. Maybe I'm more aggressive, or I lose my mind when I shift. What happens doesn't matter. What *does* matter is that I'm not willing to risk it."

"But this is the best way to try."

"What way?"

"I'm a phoenix shifter. I can shift and fly away if I need to. If you become dangerous, if you're defective or lose your mind or just aren't yourself anymore, if you try attacking me, I can go."

"And leave me alone in the woods where I could attack anyone?"

"We'll make sure to go far away where no one goes. You can't *not* find out what happens when you shift, Owen. Your wolf is part of you. You're young, and you can't live another fifty or sixty years without shifting. You're a shifter. Your animal is part of you, whether you like it or not, whatever your father says."

Owen stared at Lennox. "I thought you didn't talk much," he said.

Lennox's cheeks instantly became red. He looked away, but he didn't back down. "I usually don't, no. This is important, though. *You* are important."

Those words gave Owen pause. He was terrified, yes. He'd been taught to be terrified when it came to his wolf. Did he really have to be, though? He didn't know, and he wouldn't find out unless he shifted. Maybe Lennox wasn't wrong. Maybe Owen ought to do it like this, with only a phoenix around, in a place where people wouldn't stumble onto them. If he shifted, he would finally find out what was wrong with him, and he could take appropriate action. He could find a way to deal with his wolf and make decisions better than he could now.

The thought wasn't any less scary than it had been before, but Owen thought Lennox might be right. He didn't want to give up his new life, the life he'd been offered even when he'd thought he didn't deserve it. He also wanted to know who and what he was, though.

"I can guide you through the shift if you're afraid you won't be able to, since you haven't shifted in a long while," Lennox said. "I know it's weird, since usually, it's instinctive, but if you think you have a problem shifting, I can help you."

"It's not that, although, thank you. I do wonder if I'll manage to shift."

"That won't be a problem. I'll help you."

"You'll also make sure nothing happens and that no one gets hurt?"

"Of course. Be it a pack member or you."

Things wouldn't get better than this. Owen was aware of that, and he knew this was the best he would have. Once he found out what happened to him when he shifted, what he became, he would be able to make decisions. Maybe he would decide he had to leave. Maybe it would be the best thing to do for both himself and the pack. Whatever happened, he would know, and that was what he'd wanted since he could remember.

Lennox was worried, but he was also incredibly curious about Owen shifting, or rather, not shifting. Why had his father forbidden him to shift? Why hadn't he explained the reason behind it? It didn't make sense, at least not to Lennox. If Owen's father hadn't wanted him to hurt anyone and had wanted him to be careful when he shifted, he should have explained why. It would have helped Owen understand why he shouldn't shift, and he wouldn't be so lost right now.

Whatever the reason, Lennox didn't care much about it. The few times he'd met John, he hadn't liked him, and that hadn't changed. From what little Owen had said when they were in the car coming back, John had never been a father to him, and what he'd told Lennox this morning had solidified that opinion. He'd adopted Owen because his wife had wanted a child, but once she died, he'd distanced himself, except, apparently, when it came to shifting. From what Lennox knew, Owen's mother had died a few years back, so she might have known why Owen couldn't shift. It was a pity they couldn't ask her, mostly because Lennox wanted to be prepared. He didn't think Owen would be dangerous, but there had to be a reason why John wouldn't let him shift, and as curious as Lennox was, he was also nervous.

He hadn't been lying when he'd told Owen he wouldn't have a problem leaving if Owen became violent. Still, he didn't want to. He didn't want his mate to think he was dangerous. Even if that was the case, they would find a way around it. They had to. Besides, Lennox was used to this kind of situation. He might be quiet, but he was a phoenix shifter, and he'd traveled around the country protecting packs and other shifter groups. This wouldn't be any different, except that the person he might have to protect the pack from was his mate.

Okay, so maybe it would be different. Lennox wouldn't find out until Owen shifted, which was why they were walking outside in the forest, headed toward a quiet space Lennox often used to shift. He was part of the Rosewood pack now, but it didn't mean the pack members were all comfortable with him and his brother. They were phoenix shifters, and they had a reputation. They couldn't do anything about it, and Lennox knew some pack members were wary. Carey was aware of that, too, but he didn't care. He didn't have a problem shifting in front of them or playing around with his mates. Lennox wasn't like him. Since people were afraid of him, he preferred shifting in private, which was how he'd found the spot.

It was a clearing about fifteen minutes away from the main pack area. It wasn't hard to get there, but he knew most pack members stuck closer to the pack when they shifted, especially those with children. He'd never seen anyone here, and he hadn't smelled them either, so he was pretty sure he was the only one who used this place. If Owen tried to attack him for whatever reason, he would be able to fight back and warn the pack. They would help him get Owen under control, and they could decide together what to do next.

Lennox couldn't help but wonder if pushing the way he had might create even more problems. Owen might not know what happened when he shifted, but he was clearly terrified, and he thought he might hurt people. Lennox didn't want that to be true, but what if it was? What would they do then? Camden couldn't afford to keep someone dangerous in the pack.

He might not want to do it, but he would have to tell Owen to leave. What would Lennox do, then?

He already knew. If Owen had to leave, if the Rosewood pack didn't want him, Lennox would go with him. It would hurt, because he'd never been away from Carey, but he would deal with it. They were twin brothers, not mates. They could be without each other, even if neither of them would like it.

"This is far from the pack," Owen said.

"It is. Since I'm a phoenix shifter, I have to be careful when I shift."

"Does Carey shift with you?"

"Not usually, no. He shifts with his mates now, and neither of them will allow any pack member to look at him wrong. Besides, Carey doesn't care about those things. He doesn't care if people hate him, as long as it's not the people he loves."

"I wish I could be like that," Owen said, his voice wistful. "You're not, either."

"I don't like it when people are afraid of me, especially when I did nothing to earn it. They're afraid because of what I am, not of what I did. It's not fair, and it wouldn't be fair in your case, either."

"My father had to have had a good reason not to want me to shift."

"Maybe." Maybe not. Lennox couldn't say he knew John Harris well, but he knew the man wasn't a good person. He might just have been trying to torture his adopted son, as far as Lennox knew. He wouldn't be surprised. John was the kind of man who liked control, and it was hard to control children. Lennox didn't know why John and his wife had never had biological children, and he didn't think it mattered. Whatever the reason, John resented Owen, and that might be the only reason he'd told him not to shift. "What about the Springfield pack?" he asked.

Owen looked at him. "What about them?"

"They never said anything about you not shifting? I mean, they would have noticed."

"They had questions in the beginning, especially when I was a kid. I think John told them that I couldn't shift or something. He told them I was defective, and they didn't push."

"But you went into the woods with your friends to shift."

"I did, but I don't think my friends thought I could actually do it. They might not have been wrong. I was going to try, but I still have no idea if I can shift at all. If I ever did, I don't remember it. Maybe I can't shift, and John was ashamed of me because of that."

"You were adopted," Lennox said slowly.

"I was."

"So you could be something else."

"You mean that I could be something different from a wolf? I guess I could, but I doubt John would have adopted me if I wasn't a wolf. He wouldn't have wanted to have a child that was different."

"Possibly." But Lennox couldn't help but wonder if that was the case. They wouldn't find out until Owen shifted, but his mind was racing with possibilities. So far, it was entirely possible that Owen's wolf was defective and that John didn't want others to see it. It was also possible that Owen was different, though. Lennox wouldn't be surprised if that had been a problem for John. Maybe it was the reason he'd tried to hide it. "The Springfield pack knows you were adopted."

"They do. My mother wanted children, but she lost all of them, and that was a known fact. No matter how many times she tried, she couldn't carry the pregnancy. She was desperate for children, which was why my father adopted me."

"Where did he find you?"

Owen blinked. "I don't know. He's never talked to me about the adoption."

"But you asked."

"I wanted to know who I was, where I came from. He didn't want to talk about it, though."

"Just like he didn't want to talk about your shift."

Owen's expression was a mix of fear and hope. "You're right. He didn't want to talk about my shift, and he didn't want to talk about my biological family. You think it's related?"

"I don't know, but we might be about to find out."

This was it.

Owen looked around the small clearing in which they stood. Lennox had told him he came here to shift on his own, and Owen could see why. It was a quiet place, away from the pack, so people probably wouldn't stumble onto them. If Owen went crazy and Lennox had to stop him, he would be able to do so before Owen reached the pack.

Owen swallowed. He was so terrified he felt like he was drowning, and he didn't know how to deal with it. He'd always thought he would never shift. He'd never wanted to risk it, even though he'd been dying to find out what John's reason for preventing it was. He wanted to know where he came from, whether he was even a wolf shifter or something different. His father had never answered his questions, and he doubted he ever would. He wanted to keep Owen's animal form a secret, but Owen had no way to know why until he shifted.

Which was what he was about to do.

"This is crazy," he murmured.

To his surprise, Lennox reached for him. He grabbed his shoulder and squeezed quickly before dropping his hand, but the touch had been enough to settle something in Owen. "You can do it," Lennox said.

"What if I'm dangerous?"

"We'll decide what to do once we get you to shift back to your human form. This is the safest thing to do for everyone, Owen. Right now, we have no way to know whether or not your shifted form is dangerous. It means that if something happens and you shift without meaning to, it will make everything worse. But if you know what you shift into and what the problem is, we can deal with that. We can make decisions, try to protect you and everyone else. I know you're afraid, but trust me, it's the best thing to do."

Owen looked at the clearing again. "If I'm dangerous . . ." he began. He had to swallow to continue. "If I'm too dangerous, you have to leave."

To Owen's surprise, the corners of Lennox's lips curled. "I'm a phoenix shifter. I could burn you with a thought."

"And I want you to do just that if I'm too dangerous or if I lose my mind. Please. I wouldn't be able to forgive myself if I hurt someone."

"I'm not going to kill you, Owen."

Owen crossed his arms over his chest. "I won't try to shift if you don't promise me you'll stop me if I'm dangerous."

They stared at each other. Owen didn't want to die, especially not now that he'd found a home. He wouldn't hesitate to have himself killed if it needed to be done, though.

"Shift, Owen. We can make all the decisions once we know what's going on," Lennox said.

Owen was wasting time. He could admit that, at least to himself.

Lennox would do what was best for the pack. That was his job, the reason he'd come here in the first place. He was here to protect the pack from the Springfield pack, and from Owen if he needed to. He would do what needed to be done, even though Owen was his mate. Owen might not have known him long, but of that, he was sure.

So he decided to do it. He was going to find out why he

couldn't shift and what he was, and they could make all the decisions later.

Owen quickly stripped. He left his clothes on a tree and wrapped his arms around himself. Since he'd never shifted, he wasn't used to this. He'd never been naked in the forest, even though everyone he knew had. It was awkward and uncomfortable. He didn't miss the way Lennox was looking at him, though, and he knew it wasn't because he found Owen ugly. There was so much interest in his gaze, in the way he looked Owen up and down. He wasn't shy about it, but he also wasn't lecherous, and to Owen's surprise, he relaxed. He kept his arms around himself, but it felt easier.

Lennox cleared his throat. "Okay. This is how it works. Close your eyes."

"People don't close their eyes when they shift," Owen pointed out.

Lennox playfully glared at him. "Not when they're used to shifting, no. You'll have to focus, though."

"You think it's going to be hard?"

"Either it's going to be, or whatever animal you have inside is going to be so eager to come out, you'll shift right away. There's no way to know until you try."

Owen wasn't sure which option made him feel better, but he obeyed and closed his eyes.

"Think about your animal. Feel him inside you."

That was easy. Even though Owen had never been allowed to shift, he'd always been aware of what was inside him. He might not be able to give it a name or a form, but he knew it intimately.

He reached out, and his animal answered. It came closer, hesitant, probably wondering why Owen was doing this now. It had suffered as much as Owen, and Owen told him that it was over, that he was free.

Owen didn't even realize he'd shifted until Lennox told

him to open his eyes. He did so, blinking at the light in the forest.

At the new sight in front of him.

He wasn't standing on two feet anymore. His body was lower, which told him he wasn't human.

Lennox crouched in front of him. He was frowning, but he didn't seem afraid, and Owen took a moment to think about how he felt.

He didn't feel crazy. He didn't feel like he was about to attack Lennox. He didn't feel the need to hurt him, to eat him, or do anything like that. He was entirely in control, and that was a relief, so much so that his legs buckled. His eyes were wide when he fell on his face, but it made Lennox laugh, and it was a relief, especially after the frown.

Lennox's fingers touched Owen's fur.

He had fur.

"Okay, so you're a wolf," Lennox said.

Owen blinked. That didn't make sense. Why hadn't his father wanted him to shift if he was a wolf just like everyone else in the Springfield pack?

Apparently, Lennox was following the same train of thought. He was still crouched in front of Owen, and he kept stroking the fur on Owen's head, still staring at him, clearly thinking.

"Now, I've seen a lot of wolf shifters since I moved here," Lennox continued. "And while you *are* a wolf, you're also slightly different."

Owen frowned. He didn't like the sound of that. He tilted his head, hoping Lennox would understand. He was relieved when his mate did.

"I can't tell you if you're a different kind of wolf, or if it's something else. You might belong to another species. I don't know. I do know someone who would probably know, though." Owen continued staring at him. With a sigh, Lennox continued. "We should talk to Camden. He's an alpha, and he's bound to know what kind of wolf you are. I don't think you have anything to be afraid of, though, Owen. Whatever your father told you, you're not violent, and I can tell you're yourself. You're in control."

Owen nodded. He really was. He hadn't expected it, and it was puzzling, but in a good way.

At this moment, he didn't care that his father didn't want him to shift. He just cared about the fact that he finally had, and that he'd never felt as free as he did now.

Lennox got to his feet. "How about I shift, too? We can play around in the forest for a bit, and you can get used to this new form of yours. It's going to be a little while until you're coordinated when you move. Children usually learn this while they're learning to walk, so it will be different for you, but I'm sure you can do it."

Owen wasn't looking forward to having to learn to walk again, but Lennox wasn't wrong. He could do this. He'd shifted, and nothing bad had happened. That meant he would shift again and again until he was comfortable doing it. He'd finally embraced this part of himself, and he wasn't about to shut it away again.

CHAPTER FOUR

Lennox understood why Owen was nervous. He probably would be too, in this situation. They still had no idea why Owen's father had forbidden him to shift, and they weren't sure Camden would have an answer for them. He was their best bet, though, which was why Lennox was relieved when Owen had agreed to talk to him. Now they just had to hope Camden would be able to tell them more, and that whatever kind of wolf Owen was, he wasn't dangerous and he'd be allowed to stay with the pack.

Lennox didn't want to think about leaving, not when he felt he'd finally found a home. It wasn't just about Carey, either. He didn't want to leave his brother, but they were adults, even though they'd lived together all their life. He could be without Carey if he had to, and the same went for Carey. But Lennox liked Rosewood. Some of the pack members had been wary of him and Carey, and some still were, but mostly, they'd welcomed them as if they'd always belonged with the pack. It was easy for Lennox to imagine making this place his home, and it already was, in a way. He might not have his own home, but he didn't mind living with Camden and Toby, especially when it came to keeping Toby safe. He wanted to stay. He wanted Rosewood to become his home, to grow old here.

He wasn't sure he would be allowed to.

Camden was a good person. He would try to do what was best for everyone, but his first priority was the pack. He might hate it, but if it was necessary, he would ask Owen to leave.

That was why Lennox was nervous. He wouldn't let Owen go on his own. He'd been on his own for far too long, and Lennox knew how that felt. Owen didn't deserve it. What he was didn't matter. Hell, most people thought phoenix shifters were crazy, that they burned things just because they liked it.

Yes, phoenix shifters were dangerous, and they had the ability to set things on fire with their minds. It didn't mean Lennox did it, that he didn't want to live a simple life with friends and family. Most people didn't understand that, and Lennox wasn't about to explain it to them. It wasn't his fault they were idiots. It had been fine for him and Carey, but he didn't want Owen to go through that. He wanted Owen to have a home, to be able to settle down, to start living after he'd left Springfield. Owen hadn't given him details of his life with the Springfield pack, but knowing he'd been forbidden to shift was enough to tell Lennox it hadn't been great.

Owen's father had to pay for taking Toby from his home and kidnapping him. Hopefully, he would. But he'd also been a bad father to Owen, and the pack was supposed to be about family. Even though Owen was only in his twenties, no one had ever asked him why he didn't shift. Hell, they might not even have noticed beyond the first few times. That was what they thought of him, the way they considered him, and Lennox hated it. Lennox hadn't had a family, except for his brother, but he knew Owen deserved one. They were both orphans, even though Owen's adoptive father was alive, and Lennox hoped they could make a family together.

That wouldn't happen if they were kicked out of the pack, but if they were, they would find another way. Lennox always did, and Owen was a survivor, just like he was.

"I feel more nervous than I was before shifting," Owen said.

He was trying to appear calm, but Lennox could hear the tremor in his voice. He could see his hands trembling. He didn't say anything about it, though. Of course he was nervous. Anyone would be in his place.

Owen bit his lower lip and looked away. "What do you think they'll do? Will Alpha Cook kick me out of the pack?"

"I don't see why he should."

"I could be dangerous."

"You're a wolf. Wolves can be dangerous, but that goes for all of them, not only for whatever kind of wolf you are. I wouldn't worry too much if I were you."

"Too late for that. I'm already worried."

Lennox hesitated. He'd been the one to suggest they see Camden, but they might still be able to go back. Camden didn't know they were coming. Hell, Camden didn't even know Owen had shifted. They hadn't seen him today, and they might not see him until dinner unless they were to seek him out. "You can keep it a secret. You don't have to tell Camden about this. You don't have to tell anyone."

He could see Owen was tempted. He wasn't surprised when Owen shook his head, though. He'd expected it.

"I have to tell them. I want to find out what I am, and I don't want to put the pack in danger. They offered me a home. What kind of man would I be if I hid something like this from them? Besides, like you said, I'm a wolf. Whatever kind of wolf I am, I can't be any more dangerous than the other wolf shifters here."

Lennox hoped they both were right, but there was no way to know.

They continued walking through the forest together, side by side, their hands brushing every so often. Lennox didn't know what to do. He never knew what to do, not when it came to intimacy. He wasn't used to it. He wasn't like Carey, who'd had several serious relationships in the past, as well as a long string of one-night stands. Carey could talk people into his bed and his life, but Lennox was different. Besides, he didn't want one-night stands. They were good enough for Carey, and he didn't blame him for that, but he couldn't deal with them. He wasn't used to having someone in his life who wasn't his brother, and he had no idea how to deal with that.

He would find a way, though. He knew he would have to push himself, but he was ready to do just that.

The next time his hand brushed against Owen's, he opened his fingers and gently took Owen's in his. Owen jerked, but he didn't pull away, and after a few moments, Lennox was brave enough to link their fingers together.

It was awkward. Lennox wasn't used to holding hands, but it wasn't a bad feeling. Besides, even if it was, he would push himself. Owen needed him right now. He needed comfort, re-assurance, to know that he wouldn't be alone even if he got kicked out of the pack. Lennox could give that to him, and he wanted to do it.

Way too soon, they reached the home they both lived in. They had no way to know if Camden was inside or if he'd left for a meeting or something else, but they'd decided to go straight to his office. That was the best way to find him, and if he wasn't there, well, they would continue looking for him. If it came to it, they could wait until he came home for dinner tonight. He always did.

They didn't have to wait. When Lennox knocked on the office door, Camden's voice told him to enter, and they did. They found him behind his desk, one of his betas on the other side of it. Griffin was talking with Camden, and he nodded at them when he saw them. His gaze softened when he looked at Owen, and Lennox found himself hoping it meant everything would be all right. "Owen, Lennox," Camden said. "What can we do for you? Or did you want to talk to only me? Griffin can go."

Lennox looked at Owen. He was the one in charge here.

Owen shook his head. "I might as well talk to both of you."

That got Camden's attention, and he straightened in his chair. "What is it? The Springfield pack?"

"No. Well, not really. I have a situation, and I'm not quite sure what to do."

"Sit down. We can talk. I'm sure we can find a solution."

Owen hesitated and looked at Lennox, who nodded at him. Lennox saw him swallow, and he held his breath. He'd never been a praying man, but now, he found himself praying that everything would be okay and that Owen would be allowed to stay.

"Actually, it's probably a good idea if I stay on my feet. I have something to tell you and something to ask you."

Camden and Griffin exchanged a glance, then they both looked at Owen again. "We're listening."

"I was always forbidden to shift. You know I was adopted, Camden?"

"You told me yesterday, but I don't understand what it has to do with shifting."

"I don't know either. I just know that since I was a baby, my father always told me I couldn't shift. He never explained, never told me why. I obeyed him because I was afraid I would hurt someone." Owen swallowed loudly. "But Lennox convinced me to shift, to make sure of the kind of animal I shift into. We weren't even sure I was a wolf, not since I haven't shifted that I can remember."

Owen pressed his lips shut and seemed not to be able to continue. Lennox didn't want to put himself in the spotlight, but he would if it was for his mate.

He cleared his throat. "He shifted in the forest just now," he explained, his voice rough. Thankfully, both Camden and Griffin knew he wasn't dangerous, that he always felt uncomfortable speaking. "He's a wolf, but not quite. He's slightly different from you guys, and I'm not sure what kind of wolf he is. We're also not sure why John would have told him not to shift, since he's just a wolf shifter, and he lived in a wolf pack."

Camden looked interested, his eyes glittering. He turned his attention back to Owen and gestured at him. "You should probably shift."

"Are you sure?" Owen asked.

"That way we'll be able to see the kind of wolf you are, and we can give you an answer. Of course, you don't have to. Maybe if Lennox describes your wolf form, it'll be enough for us to recognize the kind of wolf you are."

Owen shook his head. He took a step away from Lennox, letting go of his hand, and Lennox regretted it. He didn't move away, though. He stayed as close to Owen as he could as Owen slowly stripped. It was obvious that Owen was shy, and it made sense since, he wasn't used to shifting, so Lennox placed himself in front of him, blocking Camden and Griffin's sight of him. A hand pressed against his back, in thanks or something else, he didn't know. It disappeared, though, and when Lennox turned around, the same wolf from before stood in front of him.

For the second time in less than an hour, Owen had shifted. He was grateful for Lennox's presence in front of him, blocking Camden and Griffin from seeing him. He trusted them, but he wasn't used to shifting, and he felt uncomfortable knowing they would see his naked body. He would have to get over that eventually, especially if he was going to continue shifting, but he would have time. Right now, he was more worried about finding out what kind of wolf he was, especially if the wolf was dangerous. He hoped not. Even when he was in his wolf form, he felt like his usual self. He didn't feel the need to attack people or do anything dangerous to them. He couldn't know that would continue, though.

He hoped it would.

Lennox had stepped away once Owen completed the shift. Owen found himself facing Camden and his beta, and he held his breath as they both rose from their chairs and came closer. Camden crouched in front of him, held a hand out, but stopped before touching him. "Can I?" he asked.

Owen nodded. He almost toppled to the side, but he managed to stay up. Moving in his wolf form was going to take a while to get used to, and he hoped he would have that time. He hoped he would still be with the Rosewood pack once he finally managed to be the shifter that he'd always been but had never been allowed to be.

"He's a wolf, but not quite," the beta said. He wasn't coming closer, which was a relief. Owen had never met him, and while he was sure the man was a good one—he had to be, to be Camden's beta—he was still wary.

"You're right. He looks like a wolf, but there are a few differences. I'm not sure. You know what kind of wolf he could be?"

"Maybe." The beta paused, then looked straight at Owen. "Can I come closer?"

Owen hesitated but eventually nodded. If the beta knew what kind of wolf he was, he wanted to find out.

"I'm an idiot," Camden said. "Owen, this is my beta, Griffin. I should have introduced the two of you as soon as you came into the office, but after what you told us, I was curious. I apologize."

Owen huffed. He didn't know how to communicate in his wolf form yet, and he hoped this would be enough. It made Camden smile, which was a plus.

Then Griffin was there, looking at Owen closely, and Owen held his breath. He released it when Griffin leaned back, even though he wasn't sure whether or not Griffin had found what he was looking for.

"Griffin?" Camden asked.

"What do you know about dire wolves?" Griffin asked.

Owen didn't know anything about them, but Camden obviously did, because he blinked. "They're supposed to be extinct."

"It's what most people think. I'm pretty sure your father had a relationship with one of them, though." Camden's eyes widened, and Griffin seemed to realize what he'd said. "Not that way. I meant that a small packet of dire wolves came through the territory about twenty-five years ago. They were trying to find a place where they could build their pack, could put down roots. They stayed here for a night, then they left, but I know your father kept in contact with them."

"And you think Owen is a dire wolf?"

Griffin pointed at Owen. "Look. Smaller feet than us, but a larger head. He's a bit bigger, but he has shorter legs. And I'm sure that if I were to look at his teeth, I'd find they're larger than ours."

Owen wanted to know more. He wanted to find out what dire wolves were, why he was different, and if he was dangerous. He had so many questions, and he couldn't ask any of them if he stayed in his wolf form.

So he shifted back. It was easier now that he knew how to do it. He was thankful to Lennox for telling him how to deal with it, but he was pretty sure he could have done it on his own. He was grateful he hadn't had to, though. He didn't know what would happen with Lennox, and they hadn't talked about it, but from the way Lennox was behaving, Owen was hopeful that eventually they would be together. But this was more important, at least for now. Owen had to be sure he wouldn't hurt Lennox or anyone else before he made any kind of decision.

He grabbed his clothes and put them on in a rush, almost putting his t-shirt on the wrong way around. Lennox gave him a soft smile and tugged it until he realized that, and by the time he was dressed again, Camden and Griffin were still talking. He cleared his throat to get their attention.

Camden startled, then chuckled. "Why don't you sit down? We can talk."

Owen obeyed. He was relieved when Lennox sat next to him, and even more so when Lennox offered him his hand to take. He wasn't about to say no. He might not be used to holding hands, but it was what he needed right now.

"So, dire wolves," Griffin said. "We thought they were extinct for a long time. They're prehistorical wolves, basically."

Owen blinked. "Prehistorical?"

"Our ancestors, if you will. You're considered our forefather. All wolf shifters come from dire wolf shifters."

That told Owen a lot, yet it didn't tell him anything. "How can that be? I mean, this can't be a reason John told me not to shift, can it? Are dire wolves dangerous?"

Griffin shook his head. "No more dangerous than any other shifter. Since Camden told me you were adopted, my bet is that John didn't want anyone to realize you were a dire wolf. What his reason was, I don't know, and you should ask him if you want to find out. What I can tell you from my experience with the dire wolves who passed through twenty-five years ago is that you look like a dire wolf shifter. You're rare, extremely so, but that's it. You're not different from us. I promise."

Owen slumped in his chair. He was relieved. He didn't have to go anywhere. He wasn't dangerous, he and could stay.

"How old are you?" Camden asked.

Owen blinked at his question, but he answered easily. "Twenty-six."

Griffin nodded curtly, frowning. "That would make sense. Like I said, the dire wolf pack came by twenty-five years ago.

I remember they had several children with them, including a toddler. He might have been about one year old."

Owen was pretty sure that if his eyes widened even more, they would pop out of his skull and roll to the floor. "Are you saying they might be where I come from?"

"Has John never told you where he got you from?"

Owen shook his head. "I asked him, but he never answered." And now, it made sense why.

Owen didn't know what to think about it. John had never been a real father. He was the only father Owen had ever known, though, and knowing that he might have taken him away from a loving family hurt.

"I can contact their alpha," Camden said.

Owen took a moment to wrap his mind around what Camden was saying. "The dire wolf alpha?"

Camden nodded. "If Griffin is right, I should have his number. My father had a long list of alphas he kept in touch with regularly, and I've been slowly going through it since he died. Unfortunately, many things have happened, and I haven't had the time to examine it. I'm sure the dire wolf alpha is on that list, though. If Griffin can tell me his name, I can find him and contact him, ask him about you. Is that something you would like?"

Owen didn't know. He had no idea what he wanted right now, but he was terrified.

But he wanted to know more. He wanted to know what had happened, where he'd come from. He wanted to know if John had taken him away from his family

He might never find out. The dire wolf pack might have nothing to do with him, and he wouldn't find out until he talked to them. He might not get answers, but he had to try.

"Call them."

Camden made the call on speaker. Lennox was grateful. He didn't know how anyone would react to this, but he probably needed to hear it because of the bond between him and Owen. Owen had been looking for a place to belong to for years. He had the Rosewood pack now, but it wasn't the same as knowing about one's birth pack and parents. Lennox had no way of knowing if these dire wolves were related to Owen, but what were the odds? Either way, he'd be there for Owen.

They looked at each other as the phone rang. Owen was tense, his fingers tightening around Lennox's. Lennox didn't pull away, though. This was the moment his mate needed him the most, and he wasn't going anywhere.

"Hello?" a male voice asked.

Owen jerked, then settled back in his seat. He bounced his knee and stared at the phone as if he could see the speaker.

Camden cleared his throat. "Alpha Smith. This is Alpha Cook from the Rosewood pack," he said.

There was a pause, then Alpha Smith said, "Of course. I heard about your father's passing. I'm sorry for your loss."

As far as Lennox knew, Camden's father had died a while ago. It would make sense that Alpha Smith gave Camden his condolences now if they hadn't contacted each other yet, and Camden would have told them if he had.

"Thank you. I appreciate it. I've been going over my father's contacts, and I thought I would call you, too."

"I see. Do you need anything in particular?"

Camden looked at Owen, who nodded. "Actually, I do. Griffin, my father's beta, told me about you and your pack."

"I remember him."

"He mentioned that you were dire wolves."

Lennox held his breath. He wasn't sure what he would do in the alpha's position. He wouldn't want to put the dire wolf pack in danger, especially after what Griffin had said, but Camden was an alpha, and his father and Alpha Smith had known each other. Alpha Smith could only hope Camden was like his father and that he was a good alpha and wouldn't take advantage of his knowledge of the dire wolves.

"He's right. We *are* dire wolves."

"Your kind of shifter is extremely rare."

Alpha Smith snorted. "You tell me. We are rare, yes. It doesn't mean we're useless, or that we can't defend ourselves. We had to learn. People tend to collect rare things, but we're not objects."

"That isn't what I was saying, and I apologize if I offended you. No, I was just making sure I had all my info right, because a few of my pack members need to talk to you."

"Talk to me?"

"Yes. I know this is unexpected. I don't know the kind of relationship you had with my father, but as far as I'm concerned, the Rosewood pack can never have too many allies. I would like our packs to have that kind of relationship."

"We can certainly talk about it. Your father was a friend, even though I hadn't seen him in decades. We kept in touch, and he was indispensable when it came to my pack settling down and finding a place to put down roots. I can never thank him enough, and I'm truly sorry for his death. I can meet your pack members. I will listen to whatever they have to say and see what I can do for them."

"Thank you."

Lennox turned to smile at his mate. It was the first step toward what Owen wanted, and even though it wasn't much, it was better than nothing—which was what Owen had until now. These dire wolves might not be related to Owen, but it was a step forward.

"If you'd like, I can send them to you today," Camden continued

"I'll be waiting for them."

Lennox wasn't sure about that, but he waited until

Camden hung up to ask, "What about the Springfield pack?"

"They'll probably be quiet for a while, especially after what happened with Toby. Alpha Johnson wasn't happy with what his envoy did, and I doubt he'll want to take risks, especially not this soon. But if you're worried, I can have Carey stay with us for a bit."

"I would be more comfortable if he did, yes. I don't think the Springfield pack will try to get to Toby again, but this way, I'll be able to focus on Owen."

"I'll let Carey know." Camden turned his attention to Owen. "I don't know how you feel. I've never been in this kind of situation. I can guess you're nervous, though, and I want you to know that whatever happens, you'll always have a home with us."

Owen's fingers tightened around Lennox's. "Why? You don't know me. I know I helped Toby, but I'm sure he could have escaped on his own. Hell, he kicked my father's ass without needing any help from anyone."

"You're right. We haven't known each other long, but I pride myself on reading people pretty decently. I might be wrong, but I think you're a good person. You wouldn't have helped Toby otherwise, and it doesn't matter that he could have done it on his own. He didn't have to because you were there for him, because you helped him. That's enough for me to give you a home for the rest of your life if that's what you're looking for."

"And you don't care that I'm not a normal wolf shifter?"

"I don't. I'm sure that by now, you're aware that the pack is home for more than wolf shifters. Toby is a unicorn shifter, as is his brother. Lennox and his twin are phoenix shifters, and Carey's mate is a jackalope. The majority of us are wolves, but it doesn't mean we can't live together if it's what you want. We've been doing well with the others, and you won't be any different."

Owen looked at Lennox, then back at Camden. "I don't know. I don't know anything right now."

"Take your time. Talk to Alpha Smith, find out if you might have been part of his pack at one time. We don't have to have this conversation now. You don't need to make any kind of decision this soon. Just find out who you are, and we'll be here, waiting for you if you decide to come back."

Lennox hadn't thought about it. So far, Owen didn't have anyone but the Rosewood pack, but that might be about to change. What if he belonged with the dire wolf pack? What if Alpha Smith knew his family? Would Owen want to move in with them? Would he rather live with the dire wolves than with the Rosewood pack? He didn't know either pack well, so it would probably be the same for him, but the dire wolves might be his family.

Lennox had no answer to those questions. He didn't know what he would do if Owen decided to move there, but now that he thought about it, he knew that wasn't right. If Owen moved in with the dire wolves and Alpha Smith was okay with it, Lennox would move, too. He wasn't leaving his mate alone now that he'd found him. The only way that would happen was if Owen told him he didn't want him in his life.

Hopefully, he did.

"You should probably head out," Griffin said. "I'll write down the address for you. I didn't talk to Alpha Smith as often as Camden's father did, but I still had contact with him, and I know where the pack is. They're good people. I know you're worried about that, Owen, but you don't have to. I don't have many details, but they settled down and have been thriving since then. It doesn't mean there are a lot of them, but I'm sure the pack is still growing. Whatever you find there, whether or not they're your family, they'll welcome you."

Owen nodded. "Thank you. I don't know what I would have done if I hadn't had you all to help me through this. I didn't even know there was something to help me through, not until Lennox convinced me to shift."

"Don't worry about it. Find out where you came from and let us know."

Owen was silent the entire time they were in the car headed to the dire wolf pack. Would he find his parents there? Was the dire wolf pack the place where he'd come from? And if it was, why had they given him away? Or had John taken him from them without their knowledge?

Owen had so many questions, and he wouldn't get answers until they arrived.

He felt kind of guilty for ignoring Lennox, even though he didn't think his mate minded. Lennox seemed to be comfortable with silence, and he hadn't demanded that Owen talk to him. A lot of people would have. They would have asked Owen how he felt, what he thought about the situation. Owen wouldn't have known how to answer because he didn't know how he felt.

He had conflicting feelings. On the one hand, if he was about to meet his family, the family he hadn't known he had, he was happy. He was also sad, though, because it meant that John had done something he shouldn't have. There was no love lost between them, but John had still been a father to Owen for twenty-six years.

Well, make that twenty-five.

Owen didn't remember anything about his life before Springfield pack. He didn't know how he'd arrived there, where he'd been found. He'd asked questions, but John hadn't wanted to answer them, just like he'd never told him why he couldn't shift.

Now Owen knew the answer to that question. The other wolf shifters would have realized he wasn't a normal wolf if they'd seen him. The kids might not have, but their parents surely would. Then John might have been in trouble, which in Owen's mind meant he hadn't been supposed to take Owen.

He'd kidnapped him. Owen didn't want to think about it that way, but it was what it was, wasn't it? Just like John had kidnapped Toby, he'd apparently taken Owen away from his family, and he hadn't thought twice about it. Even after his wife had died, when he could have sent Owen home, he hadn't. He'd kept Owen close, not telling him where he came from, or that he might still have a family somewhere close by.

Owen got even more nervous as darkness fell around them. The dire wolf pack wasn't far, just a few hours by car, but it felt like they'd been driving forever. Then Lennox took a turn, and they drove onto a gravel road. Lennox looked at Owen, and Owen forced himself to smile. "We're there," he said.

Lennox nodded. "We are. We can go back if you want, though. You don't have to do this now, even though Camden told the alpha we were coming."

"I want to do it now. I have to."

"Then we'll do it."

"You'll do it with me?"

Lennox looked almost offended at the question. "Of course."

"Thank you." Owen didn't know what he would have done if he hadn't found Lennox. He would probably still be on the way to talk to the dire wolf alpha, but it would be so different. He would be alone.

But he wasn't, because Lennox was there, by his side, ready to do just about anything for him. It was overwhelming, but in the best of ways. They hadn't yet talked about them being mates, what they wanted from each other, but it could wait. As long as Lennox was beside Owen, they didn't have to rush into anything. Besides, Owen had more than enough to focus on right now. He didn't know what they would find with the dire wolf pack, whether it would be good or bad, and he couldn't deal with anything else right now. But he was grateful for the support, for not having to do this on his own. He was grateful for *Lennox*.

Lennox parked the car in front of a big house in the middle of the forest. Owen couldn't see other houses like in the Rosewood pack, but that didn't mean they weren't around.

The front door opened before they could get out of the car, and an older man with white hair appeared. He waited for them there, looking at them, and Owen was sure he could feel his gaze running over his body. It made him want to squirm, but instead, he kept his head high. He looked at Lennox, who had come around the car, and when Lennox offered him his hand again, he took it. He *needed* to take it.

Together, they climbed the porch steps.

"I'm Alpha Smith, but you can call me Arvin," the white-haired man said.

Lennox nodded at him and offered him his hand. "Lennox, and this is Owen."

"Come in. I'm afraid Alpha Cook didn't tell me why you're here, and I'm very curious to find out. Is the Rosewood pack okay?"

"We had to deal with the Springfield pack lately, but we're doing fine," Lennox told him.

Owen couldn't look away from the man. Was he related to him? He wanted to ask, to blurt out all the questions that weighed on his mind, but he couldn't seem to get a word out. Maybe it was better this way. He didn't want to make a fool of himself, not when he might have just met part of his family.

The alpha—Arvin—led them to his office. It was similar to Camden's, although there was more wood. They settled around the desk, and he looked at them, clearly waiting for them to start explaining what was happening.

Owen opened his mouth, then closed it again. How was he supposed to do this?

"Owen is a dire wolf shifter," Lennox said.

Owen knew how uncomfortable he was talking, especially with strangers, so he realized how hard it had to be. Lennox was doing it for him because he wanted him to be okay and because he cared about him. He was going against his own discomfort to make sure Owen got what he wanted, and Owen would be eternally grateful for that.

Arvin blinked at Owen. "You are?"

"You're surprised," Owen said.

"I am. Dire wolves are extremely rare. I'm not aware of any other in the area."

"There are others in the country, though, aren't there?" Which meant that Owen might not belong here.

"A few packs here and there, yes. None of them around here. Where do you come from?"

"I grew up here."

Arvin frowned. "You did? Where? What about your parents? Who are they?"

Owen and Lennox exchanged a glance. Owen couldn't help but wonder how he would have grown up if he'd stayed with this pack. He wouldn't find out until he explained, though.

He cleared his throat. "I grew up with the Springfield pack."

"That doesn't make sense. They're normal wolf shifters, not dire wolves."

"I was adopted by one of them. He never told me where I came from or where he found me. I have no idea, and I don't think he'll tell me even if I ask again. The only thing I know is that he adopted me, and he forbade me to shift. That tells me that maybe the Springfield pack didn't know what I was."

Arvin's eyes widened. "How old are you?"

"Twenty-six."

Arvin slowly nodded. "We haven't lived here forever. We arrived in the area only about twenty-five years ago. On the way here, we passed through Rosewood territory and traveled close to the Springfield pack. That's how I met Alpha Cook's father." He paused and looked at Owen. "We lost a baby."

"What do you mean?" Owen asked, sounding breathless.

"Just that. We were wary of everyone, so we stayed mostly away from the packs. We stopped in the forest for the night, just the time to rest and sleep. One of our children, a one-year-old boy, got lost. We never found him. We still don't know what happened to him."

CHAPTER FIVE

When Lennox opened his eyes, he was greeted by the familiar sight of his bedroom in Camden and Toby's house. Owen had insisted on coming back last night, and Lennox hadn't protested. Owen had been overwhelmed, and even though Alpha Smith had asked them to stay and talk more, he'd almost run out of the house. Alpha Smith had explained that one of their children had disappeared on their way to what was now their pack territory. They'd been looking for the little boy for twenty-five years, and Owen was the perfect age to be that boy, which had been too much for Owen to deal with.

Lennox understood why Owen had wanted to leave. He hadn't been ready to consider that his father might have taken him away. They had no way to know what had happened, but knowing what he did about John Harris, Lennox didn't think the envoy had stumbled onto a little boy wandering around alone in the forest and had taken him home, then tried to find his parents without result. If it had only been an accident, surely John Harris would have done something when he'd realized Owen was a dire wolf. Dire wolves might be hard to find, but it was possible. Instead, Harris had told Owen to hide who he was and what he could turn into, and here they were, twenty-five years later.

Lennox got to his feet. He didn't know what Owen would want to do today, but he should be ready. He might decide he wanted to go back to talk to Alpha Smith. It would make sense. Owen had been panicking when he'd decided to leave, but now he'd had an entire night to think things through. He probably felt more comfortable with what had happened—as much as he could feel comfortable with it, anyway. Lennox doubted there was an easy way to accept that the man Owen had considered a father had actually kidnapped him, but even though they didn't know if that was what had happened, they both had their suspicions.

He wished he could do more for Owen. He *wanted* to do more for him, but he didn't know what. They barely knew each other, and no matter how much Lennox wanted to be with Owen, now was the worst time to push for that, or even to mention it.

He opened his door to go get breakfast, even though it was early in the morning and he couldn't hear anyone around the house, not even Camden, but he froze. Owen was standing there, wearing pajama pants and an old t-shirt, looking as if he didn't quite know whether he wanted to knock or run away. He blinked when the door opened, then took a step back. Lennox didn't move, not wanting to scare him. He had no idea why he was there and what he wanted, but whatever it was, he wanted to give it to Owen.

Owen cleared his throat and moved closer again. "I didn't want to wake you," he murmured.

"You didn't. I was going to have breakfast."

"It's early." Owen paused, maybe to find his words. He cleared his throat again and shuffled his feet. "I was wondering if we could go back to bed."

Lennox blinked. He wasn't sure he'd understood that right. "You want to go back to bed."

"I do."

"You also want *me* to go back to bed."

Owen smiled. "What I meant was that I was hoping we could go back to bed together. I feel lonely, Lennox."

Lennox had nothing to say to that. He stepped to the side

and opened his door wider so Owen could come in. Owen looked hesitant, but he stepped into the bedroom, and Lennox closed the door behind him.

He had no idea what was happening. He had no idea what Owen wanted.

Owen looked around, obviously curious. There wasn't much to see, though. Lennox had been living here longer than Owen, but he still hadn't made it his home. He'd been afraid. He and Carey always moved around a lot, and they never settled down, or at least they hadn't until now. Things were different with Carey finding his mate, though, and Lennox knew he could relax. It was easier said than done, though.

Owen's gaze stopped on Lennox. "I want you," he said.

Once again, Lennox was confused. "You're going to have to be clearer than that," he said slowly. He didn't want to assume.

Owen huffed and raked a hand through his hair. "I know it's stupid. I know I shouldn't rush into this. But you're the one thing I'm sure of right now, Lennox. You're my mate. I know you would never hurt me, not intentionally. I know you'll never abandon me and that you'll always be there for me. You've already shown that by coming with me to talk to Alpha Smith. I want you in my life. I don't want this to end, ever."

"It won't. I'm not going anywhere, Owen. I'm already yours, even though we haven't talked about it."

Owen stepped closer. "That's what I was talking about. You're perfect for me. You're my mate, and I want to be able to rely on you."

Lennox frowned. "You can, but I understand that words may not be enough."

Owen shook his head, moved even closer, and pressed both his hands against Lennox's chest. "You don't understand. You're the only person I trust right now." Lennox opened his mouth, but Owen beat him to it. "I know Toby and Camden won't hurt me. I know they want what's best for me. But I also know that if they have to choose between the pack and me, they'll choose the pack. I don't have a problem with that. It's the right thing to do. You're different, though. If you had to choose, you would choose me, wouldn't you?"

Lennox could only nod at that. It was what he'd been thinking just the day before, and he wanted Owen to be sure about that and to feel comfortable with him and with that knowledge.

Owen smiled. "See? I'm grateful to Camden and Toby, but I know I'm not their priority. I also know that I *am* your priority, though. I want that to continue. I want more." Then, to Lennox's surprise, he leaned even closer and kissed Lennox.

Lennox wasn't sure what to do. He kissed Owen back, but he was afraid to touch him, afraid to scare him and send him running. He didn't know how to behave, which was exactly like him, yet also not. He could fight like no other, but when it came to feelings and relationships, he was a mess.

Luckily for him, Owen didn't seem to mind. He leaned back, ending the kiss, and he was still smiling. "I'm sorry if I steamrolled you."

Lennox had to say something at that. "You didn't. I want you as much as you want me."

"And you don't think it's too soon for us to have sex?"

Lennox frowned. They hadn't talked about sex until now, but he wasn't about to say no. "I think it's as soon or as late as we decide it is. It's our decision, no one else's. If you feel ready for it, I don't have a problem with it."

Owen beamed and kissed Lennox again, and it seemed like they were going to do this now.

When Owen wrapped himself around him again, Lennox held him close. He moved them as they kissed, until the back of his legs hit the mattress. Then he slowly lowered himself on top of it, taking Owen with him.

Owen didn't protest. He leaned back, but only to take his t-shirt off. He dumped it on the floor and pressed himself against Lennox again, and Lennox sighed in pleasure. They were naked skin to naked skin, and nothing had ever felt so good.

They got frantic after that. They both wanted more, and while Lennox was wary of pushing Owen too much, Owen had none of those problems. He pushed Lennox to the mattress and climbed on top of him, stopping the kiss only a few moments, long enough to push his hand into Lennox's pants and wrap his hand around his cock.

Lennox jerked, but he didn't say anything. His mate could do whatever he wanted as far as he was concerned. When Owen looked at him, his expression questioning, Lennox nodded.

Then he raised his body so Owen could slide his pajama pants down his hips.

He didn't have to say anything. Owen obeyed the silent order, then took his own pants off so they were both completely naked. They took a few seconds to look at each other, but the tension was heavy between them, and Lennox knew it wouldn't break until they both had what they wanted.

Owen was a sight to behold, though. He'd been gorgeous when dressed, but now he was a vision for sore eyes. Lennox would never get enough of his mate, not now when he was young and beautiful, not when he aged and became a bit wrinkly. Owen was beautiful for more than his body, and while Lennox couldn't wait to explore it, he also wanted to explore Owen's brain, his mind, the way he thought.

Later, though.

Owen dropped himself on top of Lennox, and Lennox wrapped his arms around him. He held him close as Owen rutted on top of him, cupping his ass with both hands, pulling them together as close as he could. Owen made all sorts of sounds as he moved—moans, groans, whimpers that went straight to Lennox's cock. Lennox wanted so much more, but now wasn't the moment. They were learning each other, but Owen needed this. He needed to feel like he belonged with someone, and he certainly belonged with Lennox.

So Lennox let him do whatever he wanted. They would have time for more later. They would have time for *everything* later. Right now, this was what was important—their bodies, the way they fit perfectly together, the way Owen moved on top of him.

Owen kissed Lennox again, swallowing the sounds Lennox hadn't realized he was making. Together, they moved until they reached completion.

Lennox hoped this was the right thing to do. He wanted to believe it was as he held Owen close after they came. He wanted to give Owen everything he needed. Owen had felt desperate through their coupling, though, and Lennox waited, wondering if his mate would regret it.

Hopefully, he wouldn't. Lennox would be crushed if that were the case.

Owen relaxed against Lennox's naked body. He wasn't sure what to say. He hadn't thought much about it when he'd woken up early this morning. He'd just known he wanted to be close to Lennox, to feel like at least with him, he belonged. And he had. Lennox had given him what he needed, but now he wasn't sure what to do or say.

He didn't want Lennox to think he'd used him, even though in a way, he had. He wanted to feel like he was Lennox's, and like Lennox was his, and while having sex had worked, they should probably have talked about it before doing anything. It was too late now, though, and Owen took a moment to gather his thoughts—and his breath.

He knew Lennox wouldn't say the first word. He wouldn't have in a normal situation, and this was anything but normal. *No.* If he wanted to talk, and he did, he was going to have to take the first step.

He cleared his throat, and to his dismay, Lennox's arms around him loosened instantly. Lennox probably expected him to run, to leave, like he'd left the dire wolf pack yesterday.

It was different, though. He didn't want to leave Lennox's bed. He wanted to stay here forever, next to Lennox, to build a life with him. Lennox was his future. The dire wolves were his past, a past he didn't know yet. He had belonged with them at one time, but not anymore. Now, he belonged with Lennox.

"So that happened," he said. He didn't know what else to say, how to start the conversation. To his surprise, Lennox's chest jerked under him. He peeked at him, finding his mate laughing silently. He rolled his eyes. He probably would have laughed in Lennox's place, too.

He straightened, propping himself on an elbow, watching Lennox laugh. It was a beautiful sight. Lennox had seemed too serious from the first moment they'd met, and Owen was pleased that his mate felt comfortable enough with him to relax.

He waited until Lennox was done laughing to lean down and kiss him. It would be easy to get into this, to forget they had to talk, but he knew he couldn't. They would have to leave soon to head back to the dire wolf pack. Owen had promised he would go back today, and he didn't want to go back on that promise. He wasn't looking forward to it, mostly because he was afraid, but he had to. He had to find out what had happened. He had to know if he was the lost baby the dire wolves had been seeking for so long.

But first, Lennox.

"I don't regret this," Owen said.

Lennox's expression softened. "Good, because I don't regret it either."

"I realize we should have talked about it before we jumped into bed, but I'm grateful we didn't. This is exactly what I needed."

Lennox nodded. "That's what I guessed."

"I wanted to feel like I belonged with someone. I never did with the Springfield pack, mostly because of John, but not just him. It never felt like home, but the dire wolf pack doesn't, either."

Lennox ran a hand down Owen's back. "The Rosewood pack can be your home."

"I hope it will, eventually. But for now, it's not, not yet." Owen paused and looked at Lennox. "You're different, though. You're my mate. I feel like I belong with you, even though we barely know each other."

"That's because you do. How long we've known each other doesn't matter. We're mates." Lennox paused. "I'm grateful you took the first step. I wanted to talk to you, to ask you what you wanted, but I was afraid. I didn't want to freak you out, not after everything you went through yesterday. We can stay home today if you want. I know you promised you would talk to Alpha Smith again, but you don't have to do anything you don't feel ready for."

It was tempting to take the *out* Lennox was offering. Owen wanted to. He was terrified to talk to Alpha Smith again, to find out more about his past. He was afraid both of finding out that he was the lost baby, or that he wasn't.

He had to do it, though. "I don't think I'll ever not be afraid of finding out what happened. There will always be doubt in my mind, so it's no use waiting. We might as well go back and find out what happened to me when I was a kid."

Lennox stared at Owen for a while, then nodded. "All

right. We can go, but remember that I'll always be on your side. What Alpha Smith tells you doesn't matter. Who you are, where you came from, none of that matters to me. What does matter is *you*, that you're my mate and that I want you in my life."

That helped. This was what Owen had been looking for when he'd decided to come to Lennox, and he was glad he had. Lennox was right — even if he didn't belong with the dire wolf pack, with the Rosewood pack, or with the Springfield pack, he did belong with Lennox.

They were silent as they headed down the road. Owen didn't think there was anything else to say, especially not when Lennox kept touching him while he drove. He always had a hand on Owen's thigh or his hand, keeping him close, even though he was driving, and it helped Owen relax. He was as tense as yesterday, yet in a sense, he wasn't. No matter what happened, he would still have a home. It wasn't the home he was used to, but then, the Springfield pack had never been his home. Lennox could be, though. He already was.

Still, he was nervous. Once they got closer to dire wolf territory, he couldn't stay quiet anymore. He babbled, going through everything that had happened to him, how his father had brought him home, what he'd been told as a child. He'd always known he was adopted, but his father had always shut him down when he asked about his birth family. Owen had thought there was something wrong with them, but now, he knew better, and he wasn't sure whether or not he was ready to face it. Maybe it would be easier to accept if his birth family had been horrible and abusive, but somehow, he doubted it. That meant that the man he'd considered a father, albeit not a good one, had taken him from his home, and he'd probably known what he was doing.

Owen didn't have any more answers when they finally reached dire wolf territory. Still, he felt more comfortable. The silence coming from Lennox hadn't been awkward, especially since Owen had filled it with his babbling. Lennox had never once said anything against it. He'd listened, and he'd been there for Owen, which was what Owen had been looking for.

He fell silent as Lennox drove down the small road that would lead them to Alpha Smith's house. Owen didn't know what to expect, and as Lennox stopped the car in front of the house, he sucked in a breath.

"Are you okay?" Lennox asked.

Owen nodded, then shook his head. He had no idea how to answer that.

Lennox seemed to understand it. "We can leave, if you want. I know you promised to come back and that you want to find out what happened to you, but you don't have to do any of that now. You can take your time thinking about this and wrapping your mind around it."

Owen wanted to say yes, but he shouldn't. "We should head inside."

"If you're sure."

Before Owen could reassure him, the front door opened, and Alpha Smith stepped out of the house. Owen tried to read his expression, but he couldn't. He sucked in a deep breath, opened his door, and stepped out.

Alpha Smith waited for them on the porch. His eyes glinted with something that might have been hope, and Owen didn't know how to deal with that. "Do you really think I'm your lost child?" he asked instead of saying hello.

Alpha Smith didn't seem to mind. "I truly believe you are. There are too many coincidences. You're a dire wolf shifter, and you're twenty-six. You grew up in Springfield. I don't have any proof to show you, but yes, I believe you belong with us."

"I don't think I can move here. I want to stay in Rosewood."

"And that's perfectly fine. We don't expect anything from you. We understand how hard this is, but we do want you in our lives. We found you again, and we don't want to lose you."

"You keep saying *we*. Are you talking about the entire dire wolf pack?"

Alpha Smith stared at Owen for a moment, and Owen held his breath, even though he wasn't sure why.

Then Alpha Smith said, "When I say *we*, I mean your family. I mean my family. The child who went missing was my grandson."

Lennox wasn't surprised to find out how closely related Alpha Smith and Owen where. He'd started suspecting yesterday when he'd seen how emotional Alpha Smith had been. He'd obviously been trying not to show it, but it had shown, and Lennox had always been observant. He'd had to be, since he and Carey were constantly in danger.

Alpha Smith wasn't a danger, though. He was Owen's grandfather, and he obviously wanted to hug Owen.

Owen, on the other hand, was staring at him. He looked like he didn't know what to say, and Lennox didn't blame him. He'd come here expecting to meet dire wolves, to find out what he was. Instead, he'd found a family, or at least, that was what Lennox thought. Alpha Smith hadn't mentioned Owen's family yet except for the fact that he was his grandfather, but he would no doubt do it now.

Or at least, he would do it as soon as Owen reacted to his words.

Lennox was grateful that Alpha Smith didn't push. He stared back at Owen, waiting, and Lennox held his breath. Finally, Owen blinked, but instead of answering Alpha Smith's words, he reached out. Lennox knew what he wanted without asking, and he took Owen's hand, squeezing it in his.

Alpha Smith didn't miss the gesture. He couldn't have, not even if he'd been blind. He looked from Owen to Lennox, then nodded at Lennox.

Lennox honestly didn't care what Alpha Smith thought about his relationship with Owen, but since it looked like they were going to be in each other's lives, he should probably know that Lennox and Owen were mates. It was no one's business but their own, but this was Owen's grandfather and an alpha.

"We're mates," Lennox said.

Those simple words seemed to jostle Owen into saying something. "He's not going anywhere," he said, still staring at Alpha Smith.

"I never said he had to leave," Alpha Smith answered, his tone calm.

Owen nodded. "Good." He paused. "You're really my grandfather?"

He sounded so much like a lost child that Lennox wanted nothing more than to wrap him in his arms and hold him. Instead, he waited. The only comfort he could give Owen right now was holding his hand, and he wasn't about to stop. He would be there for Owen, whenever Owen was ready, whenever he needed him.

"I think I am. Like I said, there are too many coincidences."

"Can you tell me from the beginning?"

Alpha Smith gestured toward the inside of the house. "Why don't we sit down?"

Owen looked at the house as if it might bite him. "Is there someone else inside?"

"Only my wife, but I told her to stay away for now." Alpha Smith paused and smiled. "It wasn't easy. She wants to meet her grandson, too."

Owen's eyes were wide. "I don't know if I'm ready."

"That's entirely understandable, which is why I asked her to stay away. I knew you'd have questions. I can answer them right away if you want. I wanted to do that yesterday, but you left, so I didn't have the opportunity."

"I had to leave. It was too much."

"I understand, Owen. You don't have to apologize. The situation is far from easy for anyone, but especially so for you. I don't blame you for leaving. I'm glad you came back, though."

Owen didn't seem to know what to say, so he just nodded. They followed Alpha Smith back to his office, and Lennox looked around, half expecting Alpha Smith's wife to pop out from somewhere. She didn't, though, and they settled in the same chairs they'd sat in yesterday. He was still holding Owen's hand, and he wasn't planning on dropping it.

He felt a bit odd in this conversation, because he didn't have a place here. This wasn't his family, his history. He would never have a reunion with his parents. They were dead, and they weren't coming back.

But Owen was his mate. Owen wanted him there for support, and Lennox wasn't going anywhere, not until and unless Owen told him so. If he had to stay silent through the entire conversation, then he would.

It wouldn't be that different from what he usually did anyway.

Alpha Smith sat behind his desk, even though he looked like he would rather sit next to Owen. "You already know part of the story," he started. "Twenty-five years ago, me and my small pack of dire wolves came through the Rosewood and Springfield territories. We were looking for a place to call home, a place to put down roots. We wanted to buy a piece of land. We didn't know where we were going, though. I'd heard about lands for sale in this area, so we were headed here. We had to stop. We were tired, and we had to rest. So we did. Alpha Cook, the father, contacted us when he found out we were camping in his territory. He asked us if we needed help, and even suggested we could stay with his pack for a bit. We refused. We had no reason to trust him, and every reason to distrust him. Being a rare shifter isn't an easy thing to live as, and we've been through a lot."

"Lennox is a phoenix shifter," Owen said, surprising the three of them.

Alpha Smith blinked and nodded at Lennox. "Then he understands. Rare shifters are hunted. Dire wolves don't have any special power like phoenix do, but we are even rarer than them, and some people, including some shifters, like to hunt us. It doesn't happen to us anymore, not now that we have a steady home and that the pack is growing, but it did back then. That was why we were so terrified when we lost you. We thought you'd died, even though we never gave up hope of finding you again. Your name was Michael, although I made sure to tell the rest of the family that you go by Owen now."

"What happened?" Owen asked. His voice was little more than a croak, but he leaned forward, obviously interested. It made Lennox smile. He would never have this, but he was over the moon happy that his mate could.

"We were staying in the forest at night. We were sleeping in our wolf forms, and when we woke up, you were gone. We had no idea where you'd gone, and we looked for you, but we couldn't find you. We couldn't stay there forever. The Rosewood pack even helped us, but we lost your trace after a while, a sign that whoever had taken you probably put you in a car. We hoped it meant you weren't dead, that they would keep you, but we had no way to know. We didn't think we would ever see you again, although we hoped. We *never* lost hope." Alpha Smith paused. "Your mother didn't, either. She's been thinking about you since we lost you, and she'll be so happy to find you again."

Owen looked like he didn't know what to say. Lennox wouldn't know what to say in his place, either. Since Owen wasn't saying anything, he cleared his throat. "Have you already told Owen's parents about him?"

"Yesterday, as soon as you left. My daughter would never forgive me if I didn't. I warned them that you were raised by a Springfield pack member for the entire time and that you consider him your father and that you had a hard time dealing with the fact that apparently, he'd kidnapped you. I told them you might not be happy to meet them, and that they had to be ready to be disappointed."

Owen shook his head. "I won't be unhappy to meet them."

"But you also don't look happy."

Owen rubbed his face with his free hand. "Right now, I'm not sure how to feel. You're right. I was raised by my father ever since I was a child. I've always known I was adopted, but he never told me about my family, about who I was. He never even told me I was a dire wolf. Now, I know it means he took me, that he probably knew who you were and that you were looking for me, but for so many years, I had no idea. I wanted him to love me. His wife did. She raised me like a son, and I was happy with her. Even though my father—John—never loved me, I still considered him my father. I never suspected he could do something like this, that he would be capable of taking a child away from his family. It's going to take a while for me to wrap my mind around it."

"Of course. If you're uncomfortable, I can tell them to stay away, at least for now."

Owen's eyes widened. "They're here?"

That made Alpha Smith smile. "I wouldn't have kept them away even if I could have. Yes. They are here in the house. I should have told you sooner. It's a small miracle my daughter hasn't burst in yet. I guess she understands more than I expected her to."

"But she wants to meet me."

"They all want to. Your parents, your siblings, my wife. I know it's overwhelming, though, which is why I asked them to stay away."

Lennox tightened his hold on Owen's hand. He wanted his mate to know that he would be there, whatever he decided. He wasn't going anywhere.

Owen squeezed back, then looked at Alpha Smith. "I want to meet them. Please."

Owen and Lennox stood facing the office door. Alpha Smith had disappeared out of the office, and Owen was tense.

He was about to meet his family. He was about to meet his birth mother, his father, his siblings.

He would never forget his mother, though. She'd raised him, and he knew for sure that she hadn't had anything to do with what John had done. It wouldn't have been like her. If she'd known he'd taken Owen from a loving family, she would have yelled at him, and she would have taken Owen home, no matter how much it hurt. She hadn't known, though. He hadn't been her son, not biologically, but she'd still raised him lovingly, and he would never forget that. Meeting his biological mother wouldn't change it.

He was terrified. What would these people expect from him? Would his mother want him to call her Mom? He didn't know if he could. Even though it had been no one's fault, his mother was dead. She was the one he'd called Mom for so long, and he didn't know if that could change, not anytime soon.

"Relax," Lennox murmured.

"I don't know if I can."

"We can go back to Rosewood whenever you want. If you

feel too uncomfortable, overwhelmed, just tell me, and I'll whisk you away."

Owen looked at him. "Do you think I'm doing the right thing?"

"I think you want to find out where you come from. I think you want to meet your parents, but you're also hurt because of what happened. It's going to take time both for you and for them to wrap your minds around everything and deal with your feelings, but no, I don't think you're making a mistake. Meeting them is the first step toward healing, both for you and for them."

"I'm scared," Owen admitted. He moved closer, and Lennox hugged him. He buried his face against Lennox's neck, taking in a deep breath.

Whatever happened, he knew he would always have this. He would always have *Lennox*. Even though they'd only met a few days ago, Lennox was his safe haven, the place where he belonged.

The door flew open. Owen startled, but he didn't move away from Lennox. He couldn't. He peeked out of the embrace, looking at the woman who was standing at the open door. Her eyes were wide and she was gaping, and Owen couldn't deny that she was his mother. He'd been looking at her face every time he looked at himself in the mirror since he was a child. They looked so much alike that it was impossible for them to deny they were related.

A man stood behind her. He had both his hands on her shoulders, and he looked just as shocked. He, too, stared at Owen, and Owen could see himself in him, too.

He had no idea what to do. He wanted to rush to them, to hug them. He wanted to stay away — to protect himself. He was a tornado of emotions he couldn't identify, and he couldn't say a word.

Alpha Smith cleared his throat and gently pushed by

Owen's mother. "Now, everyone stay calm. I know you want to whisk him away, Marissa, but you have to give him time."

Owen guessed the woman his grandfather was talking to was his mother. He could see other people behind them in the hallway, all of them peeking. There was an older woman, no doubt his grandmother. There was a man who was probably a few years older than him. There was a younger woman. There were children, and they looked confused but happy.

All of them were Owen's family.

It was overwhelming. Owen had never had a family. He'd had his mother, and that was it. He'd never even had the Springfield pack, despite that he'd thought he belonged with them. He should have known from how he felt, but he'd tried to convince himself that the problem was his, not theirs. Maybe it had been. It was impossible to tell, and he didn't want to obsess over it, not when it was in the past.

He didn't know these people, but they were his family, and he meant something to them. He wasn't sure what, but he would find out. He would give them a chance, and obviously, they would give him a chance, too.

"Why don't we all sit down?" Alpha Smith said.

Owen had to stop thinking of him as Alpha Smith. He'd told him and Lennox to call him Arvin yesterday, and while Owen wasn't ready to call him grandfather or anything like that, Arvin was okay.

He gave him a grateful smile. "Thank you."

Arvin nodded. "It's all right. I won't deny we all want to rush to you and hug you and make sure you're never taken from us again, but we can't do it, and that's all right."

A pang of guilt made Owen feel bad. "I wish I could allow you to do that, but . . ."

"It's okay," Marissa—Owen's *mother*—said. She swallowed heavily and reached for him, but she didn't touch him. "My father told us what happened to you, how you grew up.

We understand you're confused and scared. We never want you to be afraid of us, so we'll stay away. We'll wait for you to take the first step."

Owen was relieved. He hadn't known what to expect, and he still didn't. He did know that he wanted these people in his life, though. No matter how long it took, they were his family, just as much as Lennox was.

They all sat down, and Owen could see how his parents leaned toward him, as if that was better than nothing since they couldn't touch him. The children had been sent away, but his siblings, his brother and sister, were there, both looking at him. He was pretty sure the girl hadn't even been born when he'd been taken, yet she was here, and she looked as emotional as the rest of them did. He didn't know what to do with that, and he felt the same way.

Owen's father cleared his throat. "These are your older brother, Lucian, and your younger sister, Sylvia. The children are her kids. Your grandmother is Eleanor, and I'm Dan." He paused. "Your father. Arvin told us what happened. We're relieved you had a good life, even if it wasn't with us."

"It was okay. My mother—" He stopped and looked at Marissa, who just smiled at him and nodded to continue. He didn't want to offend her, but his mother had been his mother. He swallowed and went on. "My mother raised me well. I always knew I was adopted, but I also knew she didn't care. I don't think she had anything to do with this. She wouldn't have kept me away from my family, not if she'd known."

"So it was her husband."

Owen nodded. "John Harris, yes. I called him father because he was my mother's husband, but he never cared for me the way she did. It makes sense now, of course, but for decades, I didn't understand."

Owen looked at Lennox. He needed a moment of familiarity, a moment to breathe. Lennox smiled at him and squeezed his hand harder, and Owen relaxed. He had no idea what they were doing, but he knew he wanted Lennox in his life, maybe even more than he wanted his family. No matter what had happened, they were his past. He hoped they would be present in his future, too, but he didn't need them. He'd lived without them for twenty-five years. He could live another twenty-five years without them in his life. Lennox, on the other hand, he *did* need. Lennox made him feel like he belonged, like he was complete. Like he wasn't lost anymore.

"Do you think he found you or that he took you from us?" Owen's father asked.

Owen had no answer to that. "I don't know what to think. A few months ago, I would have told you he probably found me and that he didn't know what to do with me, so he brought me home. Now, though? I have no idea. He kidnapped an alpha mate. He took Toby back to Springfield, even though he knew it was wrong. Maybe he did the same to me. Maybe he kidnapped me fully knowing what he was doing."

"You could ask him," Lennox said.

Owen blinked at him. "You think he'll answer?"

"Maybe. You have to talk to him anyway, and to the Springfield alpha. Whatever happened in the past, if we truly suspect John kidnapped you, he has to pay for it. You won't be able to put this situation behind you otherwise."

He was right. Owen needed to know. Now he knew where he'd come from, who he was. There was still a mystery in his life, though, and it was holding him back. He didn't know what would happen if he found out for sure what his father had done, but it would be better than not knowing at all.

He nodded. "I'll talk to him," he said.

Lennox nodded back. "And I'll be there next to you, if you want me to."

If there was one thing Owen was sure of, it was that he

wanted Lennox with him, always.

CHAPTER SIX

Lennox wanted to head to the Springfield pack and take care of John Harris himself. He wanted to strangle him for taking Owen from a loving family who had mourned him for twenty-five years.

But he realized that without Harris, he and Owen wouldn't have met. He was the only reason they they'd found each other, and Lennox didn't like it. Still, if he'd had to choose between giving Owen back to his family twenty-five years ago and meeting him, he wouldn't have hesitated. No one deserved to have their family taken away. Owen deserved to be loved, and Lennox was pretty sure that was going to happen now that he was back home. It wouldn't be easy for him. He wasn't used to this, and even though the people around him were biologically related to him, he didn't know them. That would change. Lennox didn't know what was next, neither for them as mates nor for Owen, but he did know that he would do everything he could to make sure Owen had what he deserved.

Love. A family. A job he enjoyed. Owen might not have been abused, but he hadn't led a happy life, or a loving one, not after his adoptive mother died.

Besides, confronting Harris was Owen's decision to make. No matter what Harris had done, he'd still raised Owen. Not well, and without love, but Owen viewed him as a father figure. He had to be overwhelmed right now, losing the one person he'd trusted for his entire life. Knowing what Harris had done, how he'd taken him away from his family, had to hurt.

Lennox kept an eye on Owen and his family the entire time they talked. He knew Owen wouldn't get hurt. The only thing these people wanted was to be with him, to get to know him, to include him in their life. They thought they'd lost him so long ago, and the fact that they'd found him again was a miracle. It didn't matter that Lennox felt out of place. It didn't matter that watching this made him mourn his family as if they'd died only yesterday. He would never be able to get them back, but Owen had. He deserved this and so much more, and Lennox couldn't find it in himself to be angry at him.

"You said you're my grandson's mate," Alpha Smith said, turning his attention to Lennox.

Lennox blinked. He hadn't expected to be pulled into the conversation. "I am."

"I can't believe he's already found his mate," Owen's mother said.

The attention made Lennox want to hide, but instead, he straightened his shoulders. "We were lucky."

"How did it happen? Do you live with the Springfield pack, too?"

Alpha Smith apparently hadn't told his family much about what the three of them had said the day before. Maybe he'd wanted Owen to do it.

Lennox looked at Owen, who smiled at him and squeezed his hand. "Lennox came to the Springfield pack when my father—" He paused and looked at his real father, who shook his head. He didn't look angry, and Lennox had no doubt he understood. Owen cleared his throat and continued, "John, the man who raised me. He kidnapped the Rosewood pack alpha mate."

Sounds of protest and outrage echoed in the room. Everyone wanted to know why he'd done it, how he could have, and even though Camden didn't want the news of his mate being a unicorn shifter going around, Lennox thought that the dire wolves could be trusted with it. They were just as rare as unicorn shifters. They weren't hunted for the same reasons, but they still shared that, and they, more than a lot of people, would understand.

"Toby is a unicorn shifter," Lennox explained. That got him some wide-eyed stares. It also made him want to leave, but he couldn't abandon Owen, even if it was with his own family. "Toby and his brother both met their mates in the Rosewood pack. Toby is Camden's mate, the alpha mate. The Springfield pack sent John Harris to Rosewood to demand one of them be handed off to them. When they refused, the Springfield pack didn't take it well. That's when Camden called my brother and me. He hired us to take care of Toby and keep him safe."

Alpha Smith cocked his head. "Because you're a phoenix shifter."

"Exactly."

Alpha Smith didn't ask for details. Lennox was surprised. People were always curious when it came to him and Carey. They wanted to know more about phoenix shifters. Either they had a lot of questions, or they ran away entirely because they were afraid. Alpha Smith and his family did neither of those. They looked at Owen, no doubt expecting him to finish the story.

"John brought Toby back to the Springfield pack, but he had to hide him, because no one knew what he was doing. Alpha Johnson had agreed to leave both Toby and his brother alone, so John's decision was only his," Owen said.

"Why did he kidnap Toby, then?" Owen's brother, Lucian, asked.

"I don't know. He couldn't have kept Toby hidden for much longer than he did. If you kidnap a unicorn shifter, it's probably because you need him to heal someone."

Those words made Lennox frown. Was that something Harris was hiding? Of course, he might want a unicorn shifter for himself because they were good healers, but Owen wasn't wrong. John couldn't have kept Toby hidden, which was why the fact that he'd taken him without Alpha Johnson's authorization didn't make sense.

"I helped Toby escape," Owen continued. "He could have done it on his own, but he was chained to the wall, and when I heard that his mate was there for him, I unchained him." Owen looked away. "I should have done it sooner, but I was afraid. I didn't understand what was happening. I still don't, not entirely. John was never a good father or a loving one, but he also wasn't a bad person." He paused and grimaced. "Or at least, I didn't think he was. I might have been wrong, though, since he kidnapped me when I was a baby."

Owen's mother reached for him and took his free hand. "Don't think about that. I know all of this is overwhelming, but it's over now. You don't ever have to go back to him."

"Maybe I should." Owen's mother opened her mouth, but Owen shook his head. "I want to know why he did it. I want to know if he kidnapped me or if he found me. I want to find out all of that and only then to decide how I feel about him. I want to be able to leave him behind if he's a bad man. I loved my mother, or rather, my adoptive mother. She was always good to me, and she loved me back. John did none of that. I don't know. I just want to know for sure, I guess."

Owen's mom nodded. "It makes sense. We're not going to stop you from going back to him. Hell, I want answers, too. I have a hard time believing someone would take my baby from me. But you're the one deciding this, Owen. You're the one who will have to live with this, who already lived with it for twenty-five years. No matter how much I want answers, you're the only one who can demand them."

Owen shook his head. "That's not true. You have as much

right as I do to go there and talk to Alpha Johnson."

"You should still do it. I'm sure you'll let us know what you find."

"Of course."

"You still haven't told us how you met your mate," Owen's sister, Silvia, said.

Owen's cheeks pinked just a bit, and the sight delighted Lennox much more than it should. "When Toby's mate came to get him back, he wasn't alone. He brought two phoenix shifters with him, as well as other people. Lennox was there to protect Toby and Camden, and I didn't realize he was my mate until much later. Toby told Alpha Johnson he wouldn't leave without me. He wanted me to go with him, and I still don't know why. I hadn't told him I wasn't happy, but I guess he could see it. When Alpha Johnson asked if I wanted to go, I said yes, and I went to the Rosewood pack with them. That's when I realized Lennox was my mate. I should have noticed it sooner, but I was so overwhelmed and distracted that it didn't hit me until we got to Rosewood."

"Have you been together long?"

"Only a few days." But to Lennox, it felt like an eternity. It felt like Owen had always been part of his life, and he hoped he always would be. He might not know what the future held for them, but of one thing, he was sure.

They would be together.

Owen was angry. He'd wanted to give John the benefit of the doubt, but he couldn't anymore. Had his father — or rather, the man he'd considered his father — really kidnapped him from a loving family? Why had he done it? Owen had a hard time believing he couldn't have found an actual orphan who needed a home. Hell, it would have been easier for him to find an orphan wolf shifter or any kind of common shifter. Instead, he'd been saddled with a dire wolf. He'd made Owen think he was a monster, that he would hurt people, and he'd forced him not to shift. He'd done all of that because he'd wanted to hide what he'd done. He'd made Owen pay, in more than one way, and right now, Owen loathed him.

He wanted to find out if John had known what he was doing. He still held hope John had found him wandering in the forest, but he knew that probably wasn't the truth. He knew his father too well. It would be exactly like John to take him, not thinking about the fact that he was a dire wolf and that people would notice. It was easy to realize what Alpha Johnson would have done if he'd seen Owen in his wolf form. Dire wolves were rare, and Alpha Johnson would have tried to find Owen's family. What John had done would have become public.

Owen needed to know. He realized it wouldn't change anything. He already had his family back. He'd already left Springfield. He felt lost, though, and as if knowing the answer to that one question would solve everything.

"I think we should shift," Owen's sister—he had a *sister*—suggested.

"Shift?"

"We've never had the opportunity to shift as a family, not with you. Don't you want to shift with us?"

Owen did, but at the same time, he felt awkward. "I was never allowed to shift," he confessed.

His family stared at him as if they didn't know what to say. They probably wanted an explanation, and even though Owen didn't want to give them one, he felt he owed it to them. If they were going to be in his life, they should know what had happened to him.

He cleared his throat. "I guess it's because John knew I wasn't a normal wolf. He'd forbidden me to shift when I was a child, and I haven't, not until recently, which is how I discovered what kind of shifter I was."

"You didn't know until recently?" Owen's brother asked.

It was going to take Owen some time to wrap his mind around the fact that he had a brother and a sister and two loving parents. "I hadn't. I thought I was a monster."

Owen's mother made a strangled sound. "If I ever get my hands on that man," she began.

Her husband, Owen's father, reached out and patted her arm. "We know, dear. You have to focus on the positives, though. Owen is here. We have him back, and while he isn't used to shifting, he can now. Think about the future, not about the past. It would only make you angrier, and none of us want that. We have Owen back. Nothing else matters."

Owen should do the same. He wanted to focus on his new-found family, on the feeling that he finally belonged. He knew it wasn't as simple as that, though. It would take some time for all of them to get used to their new situation, but he still felt like they wanted him, unlike John. It was such a difference that he didn't know how to deal with it, and he was grateful to have Lennox by his side. If everything else failed, if anything happened, he would *always* have Lennox. That much, he was sure of. They'd only been together a few days, but he didn't need more time. They might not be in love yet, but it would come, and in the meantime, they both knew they belonged together.

"What do you think?" Sylvia asked.

She looked hopeful, and while Owen wanted to say yes, it also made him anxious. The only people who had seen him in his dire wolf form were Lennox, Camden, and Griffin. Owen looked toward his mate. Lennox wouldn't make the decision for him, but if Lennox was there, maybe it would be easier for Owen to say yes.

Lennox's gaze was soft as he smiled at Owen. Then, he nodded, the gesture small so only Owen would notice. Well,

Owen and his grandfather, maybe. Arvin had been paying a lot of attention to Lennox, something that made Owen both nervous and happy. He didn't know much of Lennox's back story, but since he and his brother had left everything behind to move in with the Rosewood pack, he suspected they didn't have much of a family. He could be wrong, but either way, he hoped that his family would become Lennox's, too. If they were to be together, it had to happen. Owen didn't want to choose, but if he had to, it would be easy. He didn't know his family yet, and even though he didn't want to lose them, he belonged with Lennox.

"We'll be happy to shift with you," Lennox said.

Owen's brother blinked at him. "You'd shift, too?"

"I don't see why not. Besides, I was the one who guided Owen through shifting the other day. I think he might be more comfortable if I was there, too. Unless you have something against it?"

Owen could feel Lennox tense, and he didn't like it. He knew how most people viewed phoenix shifters, and he thought it was ridiculous. He didn't want his family to think the same way, to believe Lennox was dangerous. That was only one step away from trying to convince Owen to leave Lennox behind, and it wasn't something he was ready to do, or even to hear.

Lucian shook his head. "No problem. I was just wondering. I've heard about phoenix shifters, of course, but I've never seen one in their shifted form. I just wanted to warn you if you see me gawking at you."

That startled a chuckle out of Lennox. His eyes glinted with amusement, and Owen knew he was happy about Lucian's answer. He was, too. He might be ready to choose Lennox if something happened, but it didn't mean that decision wouldn't hurt.

They headed outside like a boisterous family. Owen's head

spun with the possibilities, with everything he'd lost, everything he'd missed, but also everything he'd just gained. He didn't know what the future would be like, but he would have Lennox with him, and of course, his newfound family. It was a lot to get used to, but not in a bad way. Owen's life had been empty until a few days ago, and now, it was full of people and love. He couldn't have wanted anything more.

Lennox leaned closer and kept his voice low. "Are you sure you're comfortable with this?"

"Not entirely, but not because of them. I'm not comfortable with shifting."

Lennox squeezed Owen's hand, which he was still holding. "You'll get used to it. Your situation is strange because you're an adult and you never shifted, not until the other day. It's going to take some time, and I'll be there with you every step of the way. And if you feel uncomfortable, we can wait and do it only with the two of us. I'm sure your family will understand."

He was right. Owen was sure of it, and that helped, too.

Still, once they got outside, he waited until all of them had stripped and shifted. Being naked around that many people made him uncomfortable, and he hoped it was something he would get used to, too. John had taken so much from him, whether he'd meant to do it or not. Owen was angry, but for now, he put that anger to the side and focused on his dire wolf.

It came out easily, as if it had been under the surface waiting. Maybe it had.

Once Owen was in his wolf form, he looked at Lennox. He couldn't look away, not when his mate ditched his clothes. Lennox noticed—he noticed everything, didn't he—and winked, then shifted. Just like the first time, Owen was in awe at the sight of the phoenix. He knew Lennox liked to play in this form, so he only took a few seconds to stare at him. Then he pounced.

Lennox flew out of reach, and Owen could have sworn he was smiling. It wasn't possible, not in this form, but it felt like it, and he knew both of them were happy.

It wouldn't last forever. They would be unhappy sometimes, but as long as they had each other, their life would be perfect.

Today had been fun but tiring, especially for Owen. Lennox could see it as he moved, as he spoke with his parents. He didn't want to push Owen into doing anything he didn't want, but he thought it was time for them to go home.

Thinking about that made him wonder where Owen would consider home now. Would it be here, with his family, or in Rosewood? They had to talk about it, and they would. In the meantime, though, Lennox wanted to protect Owen. Owen was his mate, even though they hadn't been together long. It was his duty and his honor to do everything Owen wouldn't do for himself, to make sure he was okay.

"Will you stay the night?" Owen's mother asked. She looked hopeful, and even though the question made sense, Lennox hoped Owen would say no. He wanted Owen to spend time with his family, but he also yearned for some quiet alone time with his mate.

Owen looked at him, and Lennox kept his expression blank. He didn't want to influence his mate, not when it came to this.

Owen shook his head. "I don't think so. I'm sorry, but I really want to go home."

Owen's mother was obviously disappointed, but she didn't push. "Of course. As long as you promise you'll be back soon. We have so many things to talk about, so much to catch up with."

Owen smiled at her. "I promise. I don't know when we'll be back, but you have my phone number. Feel free to use it whenever you want. All of you," he added, looking around.

"Do you think you'll move here?" Lucian asked.

Lennox held his breath. Whatever the answer, he would be right there with Owen. It didn't matter where they lived. But Lennox's job was to protect the Rosewood pack and Toby and Sam. It was what he'd been hired for, even though he wasn't just a bodyguard anymore. He was part of the Rosewood pack, just like his brother, but that didn't mean his job had changed. He'd been lucky to be able to take a few days off to come here, to take care of Owen and the situation. It wouldn't last forever, though, although with John Harris taken care of, Toby and Sam were probably safer than they'd been in a while.

"I don't think so," Owen said, and Lennox relaxed. "It's not that I don't want to, but I just moved to Rosewood. It doesn't feel like home yet, but it is home for Lennox, and I don't want to take him away from it."

"I'm sure Lennox wouldn't mind moving," Lucian pointed out, and while he was right, Lennox wished he'd kept his mouth shut.

"Maybe not, but he has a job. He protects the alpha and the alpha mate, and I don't want to take him away from that and his brother. Besides, the Rosewood pack welcomed me even when they didn't know anything about me, when I was just a wolf who wanted nothing more than to leave the Springfield pack. I'm sorry."

"Don't apologize," Owen's mother said. "You make your home wherever you feel more comfortable, and we'll deal with it. It's not that far away, and we have your phone number. Don't worry about us. Focus on your future. We're your family, but we haven't been in each other's lives for long. You don't have to take us into consideration when you make your plans."

Owen looked like he wasn't convinced, but Lennox was relieved. He'd expected Owen's family to push to have him close, but instead, they were pushing him to do whatever he was happier with. To Lennox, it was a sign they truly loved him and that they wanted the best for him.

"Thank you," Owen said. His voice was a little choked up, and it made Lennox want to reach out and hold him. He kept his hands to himself, though. He wanted to be his mate's protector, but there was nothing to protect him from here. These people were his family, and they only wanted the best for him, just like Lennox did.

It took them another half hour to finally manage to get to the car. Owen's family kept finding new things they needed to tell him about, snapping pictures, having one last hug and kiss. Lennox didn't mind. He was sure his own family would behave this way if they were still alive.

Still, he exhaled and relaxed when they finally got in the car. He was used to quiet, even with Carey in his life, and this had been anything but.

"I want to go to Springfield," Owen said just before Lennox turned the car on. Lennox was grateful he hadn't waited longer to say those words. "Now?" he asked.

"Now. I don't see a reason to wait. I want to talk to him, Lennox. I want to ask him what he was thinking, if he knew."

"You don't have to do this today, though. You're already overwhelmed."

"You're right, and I doubt anything good will come of this. I still need to know for sure, though. I think I'll sleep better at night if I do, even if I'll be sad." He paused and wrinkled his nose. "I don't think I will be. I already suspect John knew exactly what he was doing. He never loved me, and even though I consider him a father, it's only because he took care of me when I was a child. He fed me, put a roof over my head. He never gave me love, but it's something I learned to deal with a long time ago. It makes sense now, and while I want to know, it's not because I still hope. I know what he did. I just want to hear it from his own mouth."

Lennox understood. He was also curious to know why John had kidnapped Toby without his alpha's authorization. It had to mean someone in the pack, someone important to John was hurt, but why hadn't he told Alpha Johnson? It didn't make sense, but Lennox had never been able to make sense of a lot of people. He didn't understand the reasons they did things, and he didn't want to, not in this case. As far as he was concerned, whatever had been on John Harris's mind when he'd kidnapped Toby, he didn't care. He'd done what he'd done, and the reason didn't matter.

"The Springfield pack, then?" he asked to make sure.

Owen nodded, and off they went.

It was already late, but Lennox was grateful Owen wanted to do this now. It was probably best for all of them to leave the past behind as soon as they could, which was what they were doing. Once Owen knew, he could focus on his future, with his family, with the Rosewood pack, and with Lennox.

Lennox didn't know what would happen between them, but he did know they would face all of this together. Being with Owen made him feel like he belonged, something that hadn't happened in a long time. The only person he belonged with was his brother, but they couldn't be each other's life, not anymore. Carey had his mate and his boyfriend, and now, Lennox had a mate, too.

"What's next?" Owen asked.

"I guess it depends on what you're asking. What do you mean by what's next?"

"With my family. With John. I don't know what I'll do once John confirms what he did. Even though I know, I have a hard time wrapping my mind around it. Do you think he'll apologize? That he's sorry?"

"You know him better than I do. You have all the answers, even if you don't want to face them."

Owen sighed. "You're right. I don't know why he took me, and I don't know if it matters. My mother wanted a child, and John provided one to her. He's always loved her more than he loved me, and that was okay. It still is. But I know she'd be horrified to find out what he did, and I hate him a bit for that. It ruins the memories I have of her, you know?"

Lennox took his hand, squeezing it. "It doesn't change anything. She would have been horrified, yes, but she wouldn't have loved you less. You have to think about that. She didn't know where you came from, what you were, but she loved you anyway. She loved you like a son, and whatever John did, it doesn't take away from that. Focus on the positive. Focus on your mother, on how much she loved you, on how happy she would have been for you to find your family."

Owen nodded. "You think I should demand Alpha Johnson punish John? I mean, whatever he did, it was twenty-five years ago. Does it even make sense to punish him?"

Lennox had to take a deep breath before saying anything. He was angry, but he didn't want Owen to think it was at him. "I think that even though it happened twenty-five years ago, it was still a crime, and he should pay for it, especially considering what he did. He's still kidnapping people, and that just can't go on. Alpha Johnson will have to do something about it, and I hope he will."

There was a pause before Owen murmured, "I hope he will, too." It didn't solve anything, but Owen had accepted it. Hopefully, that would make the future easier for him to deal with.

Owen had been nervous the entire day, and things didn't get

better by the time they got to the Springfield pack territory. He knew he had to do this, but he was starting to wonder if he should have waited, as Lennox had suggested.

It was fear and nervousness talking. Owen wanted to confront John—to know why he'd done what he'd done, how he could have. He still had a hard time understanding, even though he knew John had done it. He wanted to know why, though, and the sooner he did that, the sooner he could leave the past behind and make his peace with it.

He had a hard time believing that making one decision, leaving the Springfield pack, had brought him all of this. If he'd stayed there, he would never have shifted. He wouldn't have found out he was a dire wolf, and Camden wouldn't have told him there was a dire wolf pack nearby. He wouldn't have found his family, and of course, he wouldn't have met Lennox. Owen's life had been flipped upside down over the past few days, and he couldn't wait to have a week or two to wrap his mind around all of it.

He wouldn't be able to rest until he talked to John, though, which was why they were here.

Lennox parked in front of Alpha Johnson's house, and they got out. Owen had been there so many times that it was easy to relax thanks to the familiarity of it. He might never have been happy here, and he might not like what Alpha Johnson had done lately, especially when it came to the Rosewood pack, but it was still home in some ways. He was going to miss it, yet not.

Owen knocked on the door, and they waited. He could feel Lennox's strong and steady presence next to him, and it helped more than he would have thought. He wasn't alone, not anymore.

The door opened, revealing Alpha Johnson. "Owen. What are you doing here?" his gaze shifted to Lennox, then back to Owen. "Have you changed your mind about living with the

Rosewood pack?"

Owen shook his head. "I haven't. I need to talk to you. It's about my father."

Alpha Johnson frowned. "I've already punished him for what he did."

"How? What have you done to him?"

"He's in the pack's jail. It's only temporary, but I thought that until I decide a better punishment, it would be enough."

"Good. Because Toby wasn't the only person he kidnapped."

Alpha Johnson's frown deepened. "What do you mean?"

Owen didn't want to go over this again, but he had to. "We should probably go inside."

Alpha Johnson looked like he might want to protest, but instead, he nodded and stepped aside to let them in.

The house was familiar, and it helped Owen relax. He knew this was probably the last time he would be here, and he was happy about it. Springfield had never been a true home, even though it had kept him safe.

"What's going on?" Alpha Johnson asked as soon as the office door closed behind them.

"He kidnapped me when I was a child," Owen said. He might as well go straight to the point.

"What do you mean?"

"You have to know I wasn't his child."

"Of course I know. The entire pack does. John and Martha adopted you when you were about one."

"And where did they find me? Where did John say he found me?"

"I'm not sure. I wasn't the alpha back then, and I never really thought about it. What's going on, Owen? What are you talking about?"

Owen should have realized Alpha Johnson wouldn't know. His father had been the alpha back then, so Alpha

Johnson wouldn't have had anything to do with the situation. Hell, he might not even have been able to ask questions. His father had been a good alpha, but he'd been strict, and he hadn't allowed anyone to doubt his word. His orders were to be obeyed, and he expected everyone to, including his son.

Owen sucked in a breath. "I was always forbidden to shift," he explained.

"I knew you didn't shift, but I never realized that it was because John forbid you to."

"It was. As long as I can remember, I've always been forbidden to shift. I didn't know why, but I thought it was because I was a monster in my animal form. I asked questions, but my father never answered. I found why yesterday."

"I'm listening."

"I'm a dire wolf shifter." Alpha Johnson was going to find out anyway. Owen was pretty sure his grandfather would contact him and have words with him, and he was more than okay with that. His grandfather cared, and as an alpha, he could push more than Owen could for John to be punished.

Alpha Johnson's eyes widened. "Dire wolf? Are you sure?"

"I'm sure. I shifted as soon as I got to the Rosewood pack. I found my family, Alpha Johnson. There's a dire wolf pack a few hours from here. They were passing through this area twenty-five years ago on their way there. They slept in the forest, in their dire wolf forms. They didn't trust anyone, and they were right. They lost a little boy. He was one year old, and he disappeared during the night. They never found him or his body." Owen swallowed. "That little boy was me. John took me away from a loving family. I want to know why, and I want him to be punished for that."

"But you were happy with us. With your mother."

"With her, yes. But not with the pack. Not with John. I was never happy after she died, which is why I decided to leave. What will you do to him?"

"First things first. I'm going to talk to him, and I want you to be here. If what you're saying is true, he deserves to find out that his son wants answers."

"I'm not his son." Not anymore, maybe not ever.

Alpha Johnson nodded and rose from his chair. He took his phone out of his pocket and made a phone call. Owen was about to see John again, and just like the house, it was probably for the last time.

It was going to take him some time not to think of John Harris as his father. No matter what John had done, he'd still raised Owen for twenty-five years. Until a few days ago, Owen hadn't thought he would find his biological family. He'd been too afraid, especially since he'd thought he was a monster when he shifted. He'd expected his family to be the same, but he'd been wrong, and now he was angry.

They heard John as he stepped into the house. He was protesting, lamenting the way he was being treated, but his voice faltered once he stepped into the office and he saw Owen. His expression went blank, and he looked from Owen to Alpha Johnson. "What's going on?"

"Owen has an interesting accusation against you," Alpha Johnson answered.

John's eyes narrowed. "What have you done?" he asked, looking straight at Owen.

Lennox growled just a little, and it was enough to jerk Owen back into the moment. He rose, but he didn't move closer to his father. "I found my family. The real one, the one you took me from."

John looked frozen for a moment. Then he shook his head. "I have no idea what you're talking about."

"I'm a dire wolf. That's why you always forbid me to shift. You didn't want anyone to find out. You kidnapped me. You kept me away from my family for twenty-five years. Why?"

Owen expected John to insist he hadn't done anything. He

was relieved when it didn't happen. "Because Martha wanted a child. Why else?"

"You didn't have to kidnap me for that. You could have found a child another way, adopted one. Why did you have to take me from my family?"

"Because it was too good to be true. She had another miscarriage that night, and she kicked me out of the house. She wanted some time alone, and I was okay with giving her that. I knew how much she wanted a child, and I hated that I couldn't give her one. That's when I stumbled onto you. You were playing, and you were alone."

"Don't bullshit me. I don't believe for one second that you just found me in the woods and decided to take me home."

John hesitated. "I did find you. I caught you, and that's when I noticed the other wolves. They were far away. They would have woken otherwise, but they didn't. It was obvious you'd woken up early and had decided to play while you waited for them. So yes. I took you away. If they couldn't be bothered to keep an eye on you, then they didn't deserve you."

"Because you did? You never wanted me."

"I didn't. It didn't matter, though. Martha had what she'd always wanted. She had a child, a boy, and she was happy."

Owen couldn't do this anymore. He hadn't expected anything different, but it still hurt to hear.

"That's enough," Alpha Johnson snapped. "I don't know why I'm surprised at this, John. Lately, you've been behaving unreasonably, and apparently, it's nothing new. You're going back to your cell, and you'll wait there until I make a decision. I don't take kidnapping lightly, especially not when it comes to an alpha mate and a child."

John didn't protest as he was led away, and Owen was grateful. He had what he'd come for. He felt drained, though, as if he could sleep a week, and he was certainly going to try.

"You okay?" Lennox asked, his voice soft but strong.

Over leaned against him. "I'll be fine."

"I'll take care of John," Alpha Johnson promised.

"Good. I suspect my grandfather will want to know what's going to happen to him," Owen told him. When Alpha Johnson blinked at him, he explained, "He's the alpha of the dire wolf pack."

Alpha Johnson swore. "Not only did John take a dire wolf child, but he kidnapped the alpha's grandchild?" He shook his head. "I don't know what he was thinking. I don't know what my *father* was thinking, if he knew about this, but he had to suspect. I'm sorry for what happened, Owen. I know that nothing I can do or say will change this, but I can promise you John will pay."

That was all Owen wanted. Now that he knew it would happen, he could finally focus on his future, and hopefully, leave the past behind once and for all.

CHAPTER SEVEN

When Lennox opened his eyes, Owen was wrapped around him. It was going to take Lennox some time to get used to not waking up alone. It had only been a few weeks, and he still wasn't, but that didn't mean he didn't wake up happy every day.

He did. He'd never thought meeting his mate could make him feel like this. He'd seen it with Carey, of course, but he'd put it off as Carey being Carey. Instead, he now knew that having your mate by your side, going to bed with him every evening and waking up to him wrapped around you every morning, truly made a difference. He was happy. He hadn't thought he would ever have this—a place where he belonged, a home, a family, and of course, Owen.

They still lived with Camden and Toby, and as far as both of them were concerned, it wouldn't change for a bit. Camden was still nervous about Toby being left alone, no matter how many times Toby told him he was okay. Toby was strong-willed, and he didn't like being coddled. Lennox agreed with Camden, though. Until they were sure no other pack would try to take one of the unicorn shifters, they had to be careful, especially since they still didn't know why John Harris had kidnapped Toby.

Owen was also still getting used to being with the Rosewood pack. He didn't know what he was going to do with his life, but he had time. He was dealing with having found out that he had a family after all, and that wasn't easy. He'd crashed hard after the two days they'd spent with the dire wolves, and more importantly, after confronting his father. They still hadn't heard from Alpha Johnson, but Lennox suspected they would soon, and then things would really change for Owen. He would know what John's future would be, and he would be able to make decisions of his own.

In the meantime, this was good. This was *perfect*.

"Why do you always wake up so early," Owen mumbled against the skin of Lennox's neck.

Lennox shivered and stroked a hand down his mate's naked back. "I'm used to it."

"But you don't have to get up early. What time is it?"

Lennox peeked at his phone, then chuckled. "Not yet seven."

Owen groaned and buried himself closer to Lennox. "This is *not* natural. People shouldn't be allowed to get up at six in the morning."

"I didn't say it was six. I said it was not yet seven. It closer to seven than six, though."

"Still. It has six in it. It's too early."

Lennox was smiling, just like he'd been almost every day since he met Owen. They were still trying to figure things out, but he knew where they stood when it came to their relationship—they were together, and that wasn't going to change, whatever happened. It didn't matter where they lived, what they did for a living. They were a unit. It was them against the world, and Lennox couldn't have been happier. "I can get you coffee," he suggested.

That got him the reaction he'd expected. Owen tilted his head and opened one eye to look at him. "Is it coffee the way you like it or the way I like it?"

"I wouldn't make you drink my coffee."

"Thank God, because that is *not* coffee. It's sugar with a bit of coffee in it."

Lennox laughed, something he'd been doing more often

lately. He didn't know if it was Owen or finally having a home, and he didn't think it mattered. "My coffee is perfectly fine the way I drink it," he said.

"Again, that is *not* coffee."

"Coffee tastes like that if you don't add sugar and milk."

"Coffee tastes like coffee if you don't do that." Owen rolled away and stretched. Lennox kept his gaze on him, enjoying the spectacle. He wanted to move Owen closer again, to kiss him and maybe cuddle some more, possibly have a bit of morning sex, but Owen's stomach rumbled loudly.

"I think I might be hungry," Owen said.

"I could have guessed that."

"It's not my fault you wake my stomach up too early."

Lennox shook his head. "Come on. We can head to the kitchen and have breakfast."

"The kitchen will be empty, and that means no coffee. I'm sure Camden and Toby have better things to do on a Sunday morning than to wake up at six-thirty and have breakfast."

No matter how much Owen complained and grumbled, he was out of the bedroom, along with Lennox, ten minutes later. They made their way to the kitchen, holding hands.

That was new, too. Even when he'd had relationships—which hadn't happened often—Lennox had never been touchy-feely. He'd kept himself separate from whoever he was with, and for good reasons. A lot of people were wary of him, and those who weren't saw him like something and someone they could use. Even those who had really cared about him, he hadn't grown close to.

Owen was different. He was *Owen*, of course, but he was also Lennox's mate, and Lennox knew it was a big part of why he felt comfortable with him. Owen wouldn't hurt him. Not only wasn't he the kind of person who would do that, but he would never hurt his mate. Lennox had been lucky, and some days, he still couldn't believe how much.

When they walked into the kitchen, Lennox was surprised to see Camden was at the table, sipping coffee. For all that Owen had complained, he'd been right about one thing. The alpha didn't usually wake up this early on Sundays.

Camden looked up and smiled, but Lennox could see the tension in his expression. "Good morning. I didn't expect to see you this early," he said.

Lennox shrugged. "I woke up, and Owen wanted to come with me."

"Coffee is already in the pot."

Something told Lennox they were going to need it, so he headed there while Owen sat at the table in front of Camden. He got two mugs and filled them, doctored the coffee the way he and Owen liked it, then went back to his mate, placing his mug in front of him. He sat next to Owen, wrapped his hands around the mug, and looked at Camden. "What happened?"

Camden sighed. "I can't say this is how I wanted to start my Sunday." He looked at Owen. "Alpha Johnson called me this morning."

Owen blinked. "This morning? When did he call you? At five?"

"More like four-thirty, but yes. He wanted me to know that John Harris was executed."

Lennox let go of his mug and reached for Owen. He didn't know how his mate would react, but he wished Camden had been more diplomatic.

Owen blinked at him. "Executed?"

Lennox couldn't read his tone of voice, and he wished he could.

"For kidnapping both Toby and you. I'm sorry, Owen."

Owen nodded, then shook his head. "I didn't expect that," he murmured.

Lennox had. He'd known Alpha Johnson couldn't let this go, not with what John had done. He had kidnapped an alpha mate and a child, the grandson of another alpha. He had to have known this would happen eventually, yet he'd done it anyway. Lennox still didn't understand why he'd taken Toby, and he doubted they would now. He didn't think it mattered, either.

Owen's shoulders slumped, and he leaned against Lennox. "I don't know how to feel about this," he confessed. "I'm not happy a man died, but I understand why he deserved it. He did horrible things, even though he didn't hurt Toby or me. He probably would have continued to do whatever he wanted if he got away with it."

"Take your time to mourn him," Camden said. "He might not have been a great father, but that doesn't mean he wasn't a father to you. I understand this isn't easy for you."

"You're right. It's not. But at the same time, I'm relieved. I won't ever have to deal with him again. I won't have to keep thinking about what he did."

Lennox didn't know if that would be the case, but whatever happened, whatever Owen decided, he would be there for him. He pulled his mate even closer and kissed the top of his head. "Let go," he murmured, and Owen obeyed, pressing his body against this. They normally wouldn't do this at the kitchen table, but Lennox doubted Camden would care.

Lennox held Owen. Owen didn't cry, but he stayed still, his face buried against Lennox's chest. It would take some time for Owen to get used to it. Lennox was relieved he would never have to go back, though. What John Harris had done had been wrong, and he'd known it. Like Camden had said, he'd probably expected something like this would happen, but it hadn't stopped him. He'd gotten what he deserved, and the only reason Lennox felt sorry for him was Owen. He'd lost someone he'd considered his father.

He'd also found a family and a mate. It would take him some time, but he'd make it through. He had all the support in the world. He had Lennox, and together, they could get over all of this and be happy.

You may also enjoy the following from eXtasy Books Inc:

Blue Fire
Catherine Lievens

Excerpt

Orran saw the egg drop to the ground. He roared, making several of the humans jump, including the one who had been holding the egg. Then, he threw himself toward it. He needed to get to the egg. He needed to get it back.

It wasn't that easy. Everyone around him was fighting. The humans were afraid of dragons, but that didn't mean they would stop. If anything, having so many dragons here at once, especially adult ones, could turn to their advantage if they managed to kill even one of them. The survivors would be able to sell off the fallen's body in pieces.

Orran wouldn't allow that to happen.

When two humans rushed toward him, he swiped his tail at them and threw them against the closest wall. One of them didn't get up. The other did, but it seemed like he wasn't going to come for Orran again. Instead, he eyed the opening of the alley and tried to sneak that way, but Octavia thumped her tail right in front of him and roared in his face.

Orran turned his attention back to the egg. He leaned down

to grab it with one of his paw, but someone got there before he did.

The same human who had been holding it earlier grabbed it with both his hands and pulled it against his chest.

Orran roared. The sound made everything vibrate around them. Human cities weren't made for dragons, and the alley was tiny, so small that Orran would have trouble getting back into the air. He didn't care right now, though. He stood in front of the human and lowered his head to look him in the eyes. He wanted to tear the humans head off, but he knew better. He needed to make sure the humans hadn't hurt the egg.

The human stayed where he was. His eyes were wide and his face ashen, and he was looking around the alley, no doubt trying to find a way to escape. He couldn't, though. Orran wouldn't allow him to run away. He needed to get the egg back, but when he reached for it again, the human shook his head and took a step sideways as if trying to walk around Orran.

Orran huffed. He didn't have time for this. The last thing he wanted was to shift. Humans weren't aware that dragons weren't merely animals, and Orran didn't want any of them to find out, but it seemed this was where the situation was going. He needed to be fast, though, so only this human would see him.

He looked around. All the humans were busy fighting, so he doubted they would notice if he shifted. The pros outweighed the cons, no matter how much he disliked this, so he decided it was the best thing he could do.

He shifted. He hadn't thought it possible, but the human's eyes went even wider. He looked Orran up and down, opened his mouth, and croaked.

Orran ignored him and reached out. "Give me the egg," he said.

That seemed to get the human's attention again. He shook his head, then took a step back. "Don't touch it."

"I don't care what you intended to do with it. It doesn't belong to you."

The human's expression shifted. Unfortunately, Orran wasn't used to being with humans, and he had no idea what it meant. "I know it doesn't belong to me," the human said. "How do I know it belongs to you, though?"

Orran snorted. "I'm a dragon. You know it belongs to me."

The human looked down at the egg. "So? Even if you're a dragon, I can't know that it's your egg. How am I supposed to make sure of that? Besides, you're a guy."

Orran had no idea what that had to do with anything. "I'll kill you," he said, his voice dark and steady. "You had no right to steal the egg. You have no right to kill and hurt us and to invade our home."

The human shook his head frantically. "You don't understand. I didn't steal the egg. I was trying to rescue it from my boss."

"Nice try, but as far as I can see, you're the one holding it. You're the one keeping it away from me. You have to give it to me."

It wasn't going anywhere. Orran waited, but the human didn't seem to change his mind. "I'm sorry. I can't give it to you. I can't be sure it really is your egg, and after what just happened, I'm not going to trust anyone, not even you," the human said.

Orran shifted back. If he couldn't talk sense into the human, maybe he would be able to scare him.

The human squeaked when Orran lowered his head so close to him that he could feel the human's breath on his snout. There was nowhere for him to go. His back was against the wall, and they were at the end of the alley, so he couldn't sneak away. They could stay here forever, or at least until the human gave Orran the egg. The human, on the other hand, was going to want to leave eventually. Either that, or he'd faint. He looked like he might be about to.

Something heavy hit Orran's side, and he roared. He

turned to face whatever had touched him and realized that while he and the human had been talking, more humans had appeared. The dragons had always been outnumbered, but it hadn't mattered because they were dragons. Now, though, it looked like it might become a problem.

Orran couldn't lose the egg, and he wasn't about to leave any of his friends in the humans' hands. He knew what would be done to them if that happened, and death was preferable to that. He turned toward the human again, but the man still looked resolute. He wouldn't give Orran the egg, and that meant that Orran would have to grab both of them. It would be faster than trying to talk the human into doing this. He could always deal with the man later, once the egg was safe.

We're leaving, he projected to the members of his team.

You have the egg? Morven asked.

Not yet, but I'll have it when we take to the air. Go, he ordered.

Then, he reached out, wrapped his paw around the human, and rose in the air.

The human screamed. The screech hurt Orran's ears, but he ignored it as he and his four team members rose as high as they could. The humans in the alley were shooting at them, trying to take them down, but it would take more than that to hurt a dragon.

And the humans had more than that. Orran's eyes widened when he saw one of them take out the biggest gun he'd ever seen. He had no idea what it could do, but he could too easily imagine. Scatter! he yelled through the mind bond he shared with the other dragons.

They obeyed without protesting, and it was a good thing. The human holding the gun had started shooting, and Orran knew he was lucky to be far enough away that he wasn't hit. Even though normal bullets didn't usually hurt dragons, this looked like it would do some damage, and he couldn't allow that to happen. He finally had the egg back, albeit along with a human. He needed to get back to the palace. What do we do? Morven asked.

Fly away. We should probably separate so they don't try to get us at the same time. We'll meet again in a few hours, once we're sure they're not following us.

Got it. See you soon.

Orran snorted to himself and flew away from the alley, and from the city in which they'd found the egg. The human was wriggling in his hold, but Orran ignored it. It was easy. The human was light, but he was carrying the future of their clan, and Orran needed to be careful. He couldn't drop the human and the egg. He had no idea what he would do with a human, but he would find something.

If things came to that, he could always kill him.

ABOUT THE AUTHOR

Catherine is the creator of several series, most of them paranormal, including the Whitedell Pride Series and the Gillham Pack Series. While she graduated in translation, she decided to go the writer's way because it was more fun to create her own stories and characters.

She's been living in Italy for more than twenty years, but she's a daughter of the North—Belgium to be precise—and she misses it so much that she's already planning to move back.

She loves pizza—probably too much—her son, her pets, and of course, books. She sneaks some reading time into her schedule every time she has five minutes free from writing, demands from her various pets and son, and lastly, housework.

Connect with her:

lievens.catherine@gmail.com
BookBub: https://www.bookbub.com/authors/catherine-lievens
Website: https://authorcatherinelievens.com/
Facebook: https://www.facebook.com/catherine.lievens.9
Facebook Group: https://www.facebook.com/groups/411788002341528/
Twitter: https://twitter.com/authorCLievens
Newsletter: http://eepurl.com/c-uvKn

www.ingramcontent.com/pod-product-compliance
Lightning Source LLC
Chambersburg PA
CBHW060633130626
46555CB00002B/781